THE FINAL SHOT

Also available in this series from NEL:

No 1 EDGE: THE LONER
No 2 EDGE: TEN THOUSAND DOLLARS AMERICAN
No 3 EDGE: APACHE DEATH
No 4 EDGE: KILLER'S BREED
No 5 EDGE: BLOOD ON SILVER
No 6 EDGE: THE BLUE, THE GREY AND THE RED
No 7 EDGE: CALIFORNIA KILLING
No 8 EDGE: SEVEN OUT OF HELL
No 9 EDGE: BLOODY SUMMER
No 10 EDGE: VENGEANCE IS BLACK
No 11 EDGE: SIOUX UPRISING
No 12 EDGE: THE BIGGEST BOUNTY
No 13 EDGE: A TOWN CALLED HATE
No 14 EDGE: THE BIG GOLD
No 15 EDGE: BLOOD RUN

The Final Shot

GEORGE G. GILMAN

NEW ENGLISH LIBRARY
TIMES MIRROR

for
S.R.
a girl who knows her rights

A New English Library Original

*

FIRST NEL PAPERBACK EDITION APRIL 1975

*

NEL Books are published by
New English Library Limited from Barnard's Inn, Holborn, London, E.C.1.
Made and printed in Great Britain by Hunt Barnard Printing Ltd., Aylesbury, Bucks.

45002270 6

AUTHOR'S NOTE

This is the final book in the Civil War sequence of Edge stories. As in previous books of this type, a large part of the novel is devoted to the experiences of Captain Josiah C. Hedges against a backdrop of the War Between The States. Although complete in itself the book does conclude the sequence (in chronological order): *Killer's Breed*, *The Blue, The Grey And The Red*, *Seven Out Of Hell*, *Vengeance Is Black*, *The Biggest Bounty* and *Blood Run*.

CHAPTER ONE

THE sun crested the high peaks of the Funeral Mountains and shafted down over the foothills to bring the first promise of a new day's heat to Death Valley. It shone brightly through the east-facing window of the stage line way station and woke Dan Hochman. A grey-haired, bearded old-timer in his early seventies, Hochman greeted the new dawn with a cough, a curse and a spit. The tobacco-coloured globule of saliva missed the brass spittoon and started to dry into a fresh stain upon many old ones.

Hochman climbed stiffly out of the stinking bed and hunted around the filthy, all-purpose room for his eye-glasses. He did some more cursing until he found the spectacles on the scarred table littered with the remains of yesterday's eating and drinking. Two empty bottles – one had contained whiskey, the other pulque – a dirty glass, a coffee pot, a tin mug, chunks of stale sourdough bread and a cracked plate that was rancid with the congealed leavings of a meal of beef stew.

With the wire-framed spectacles firmly set across the bridge of his nose, Hochman was able to unscrew his weak blue eyes and see his squalid surroundings in fuzzy detail. He showed no reaction for there was nothing abnormal about the combined bedroom, living room and kitchen that comprised one half of the way station's main building. The old-timer had held down the job as manager of the Funeral Mountains way station for fifteen years. At first the whole place had been kept spick and span, but only because Mrs Hochman had been a houseproud woman. She had died of a rattle-snake bite ten years previously and since then her widower had confined his cleaning chores to the passengers' rest room and the stables.

Able to see reasonably clearly through the finger-marked lenses of the spectacles, he began his daily routine – which had never varied from that grief-stricken morning when he buried his wife. He put fresh kindling on the embers in the stove, filled the coffee pot and set it to heat. Then he dressed in boots, levis and checked shirt over the dirt-and-sweat stiffened underwear in which he had slept. These top clothes, although old and patched, were reasonably clean: for two stages – one eastbound and the other headed west – halted daily at the way station for fresh teams, and the company insisted Hochman made some concessions for appearance stake. He went out to the privy to relieve himself, squinting against the bright sunlight and not bothering to look around him.

There was nothing new to see after fifteen years, he told himself. To the east, north and south the barren peaks and ridges of the mountain range with the stage trail cutting a tortuous route across the broken terrain on a line of least resistence. West was the equally barren foothills above the vast, desolate expanse of sand ridges, salt flats and rocks spread across the deep floor of Death Valley. If there had been a wind in the night – and Hochman's drunken sleep had been too enveloping for him to know – some sand would have shifted. That would be all. So Hochman returned to the squalour of his room without even a glance around; and thus failed to see the man leading his horse towards the way station from the north.

Inside, the heat was building fast: from the fire in the stove and the effect of the now fully-risen sun beating on the roof and walls of the way station. Hochman dampened a piece of cloth to rub the sleep from his eyes and used a comb to rid his tangled beard of pieces of stale food. He chewed tobacco until the coffee pot boiled then left the ugly wad on the littered table while he drank two mugs of the bitter brew. The coffee went a long way to unfogging his brain from the effects of a hangover. The wad of tobacco had dried but he soon got it moist again in his slack mouth as he went out into the rest room to unbolt the station's front door.

There had been a night wind, for sand and grit had blown in through the crack at the foot of the door. Hochman cursed and opened the door and two windows, then started to cough again as his sweeping raised dust. He brushed the invading dirt back where it had come from without lifting his dull-eyed gaze from the ground. So he did not see that the man leading the horse had reached the stage trail where it curved towards the way station, a half mile distant.

But he could not fail to hear the shot. It cracked out with shocking clarity, splitting the perfect silence that had previously been clamped over the mountains and valley. He had returned the broom to the closet and was thinking sourly that he now had to attend to the horses. For long moments, as the sound of the shot diminished through a series of echoes, he thought his imagination was playing a trick on him. Since death had robbed him of his wife, he alone had been responsible for man-made sounds in this desolate patch of country between dawn and the time the morning westbound stage came through. So it was natural that Hochman – a little crazed by loneliness – should take a while to adjust to this violent break in his routine.

Then, fearfully, with tobacco juice spilling from the corner of his mouth, he went to a window and peered through. He saw the man and the horse for the first time, now no more than five hundred yards out along the trail curving in from the north. And getting no closer, for the horse was spread out on its side and the man was half-crouched over it, rifle still aimed from the shoulder at the animal's head. Then, while the horse remained as unmoving as only a dead thing can be, the man straightened and canted the rifle across his shoulder. Had Hochman seen the approach of the stranger and his horse earlier, he would also have seen the group of a half-dozen buzzards circling high on the overhead thermals. Now the big birds swooped gracefully down and became ugly and ungainly as they perched on rocky outcrops: waiting.

The man who had shot his horse eyed the birds for long moments and there was a rigidity in his attitude. But then the tension drained out of him as he stooped over the saddle, bedroll and bridle he had removed from the animal before killing it. He slid the rifle into the boot, then hefted his gear up on to a shoulder and began to trudge towards the way station.

Hochman chewed his tobacco fast, spilling more juice to stain his beard as an expression of anxiety added new creases to his deeply-scored, dirt-grimed face. He even considered hurrying back into his room to get the ancient Volcanic carbine which he kept under the bed. But, just before he started to turn away from the window, he cursed himself for a fool. The horse must have been lame. The rider had nursed his animal along, maybe hopeful of reaching a town that contained a horse doctor. Instead, he had reached the way station so had put the animal out of its misery. What was there in that to scare a guy? Except, maybe, the appearance of the man who kicked up dust as he walked slowly down the trail. And that only because, to Hochman, this was unique. In all his years on the job, nobody had ever come to the way station except on a stage.

Still anxious, Hochman moved to the open doorway and stepped out on to the porch which was shaded from the direct glare of the sun. He sensed that the stranger had spotted him but there was no change in his steady progress towards the way station. At first, because of the weakness of his eyes, Hochman saw only a blurred form, gaining the impression of a tall, lean frame. But, as the gap across which he looked was narrowed, he saw the man in more detail.

Tall, certainly: at least three inches over six feet. And lean as opposed to thin, with a lot or muscle knotting the flesh tight-packed to the towering frame. He weighed maybe two hundred pounds, not an ounce of it soft fat. His dress was subdued – riding boots, levis, shirt and neckerchief all black sprinkled with the grey of trail dust. The low-crowned, wide-brimmed hat grey anyway, stained dark above the band by sweat. A gunbelt slotted with bullets supported a holster tied down to his right thigh. The butt of a Frontier Colt jutted from the holster. Like his clothes, his gun was far from new. But, as he halted six feet from Hochman, the old-timer saw that the stranger's face showed more signs of long use than any other aspect of his appearance.

It was the face of a man who could be any age from late thirties to late forties. It was a long face, framed by thick black hair that reached down from under his hat to brush his shoulders. Like an Indian, Hochman thought fleetingly. But this guy wasn't an Indian. Not even a 'breed'; although neither was he a full-blooded white American. Leathery skin, lined by hardship and suffering and burnished to dark brown by sun, wind and ancestry. A broad forehead, aquiline nose, high cheekbones, wide mouth and firm, strong-looking jawline. All these features were dominated by ice-blue eyes which surveyed the world from between heavily-hooded lids. Part Mexican, Hochman decided. One parent from north of the Rio Grande, the other from the south.

As he reached this conclusion, the old-timer realised why he had been afraid at first sight of the man. It had nothing to do with the fact that he had approached the way station like no other before him. Rather, it was that the man was like no other. He was big and he looked mean, but neither was it simply this. Hochman had seen countless stage passengers who fitted such a description. No, this man had something else about him that had frightened Hochman from long range and now caused him to bunch his hands into fists to keep them from shaking, and to chew the tobacco more frantically than ever in order to keep his mouth from drying up. An indefinable aura which warned that death was never far behind when this man approached.

It took a great effort for the old-timer to tear his gaze away from the trap of the cold eyes and peer out along the trail. Wings beat the hot air as the buzzards thrust up from their perches. The big birds swooped across the intervening space and settled upon the horse carcase, screeching at each other as talons and beaks attacked the meat.

'He was a good horse,' the tall man said flatly.

Hochman watched the scene down the trail for a moment longer, as the vicious beaks tore strips of blood-dripping meat from the carcase, then looked back at the stranger. 'Went lame, uh?'

The man moved towards the porch and stepped up on it. Hochman backed in through the doorway. 'Winded was all. And I'm saddle sore. Didn't reckon I'd be able to sell him here. When's the next stage to Monksville, feller?'

In the shade of the rest room, the man didn't look quite so threatening. He dumped his gear on one of the benches and sat down gratefully beside it, pushing his hat on to the back of his head.

'Ten o'clock.'

'Place I can wash up and get a shave?' He rasped the palm of a dirty hand across his jaw, stubbled with at least three day's growth of beard.

'Ain't no part of the stage line's service here, mister. Just got this room for folks to wait while we change the teams.'

The tall man nodded towards the door at the back of the room. 'Where does that lead to, feller?'

'My room. It's private. No one's allowed back there 'ceptin' for me. Stage line rules.'

The tall man got to his feet and by an almost imperceptible narrowing of his eyes and thinning of his mouthline became more menacing than ever. 'Been a long time since I set much store by rules, feller. So I'd be obliged if you'd bend yours a little. Be a trifle riled if you don't.'

He halted halfway to the doorway and looked inquiringly at Hochman. The old--timer licked his lips and spilled more tobacco juice into his beard.

'Pretty messy back there, mister. I ain't had no time to clean up this mornin' yet.'

'Me neither, which is why I'm asking.'

'Go ahead,' Hochman allowed with a shrug.

The tall man moved to the door and went through. His expression did not alter at the sight and stench that greeted him.

'You can't say I didn't warn you,' Hochman growled.

'You hear me complaining, feller?'

The old-timer blinked, shook his head and shrugged his

thin shoulders again. 'Guess not. Help yourself to whatever you want, mister.'

'Usually do.'

Hochman sat on the rumpled, evil-smelling bed and watched as the tall man filled a pan from a water pitcher and set it on the stove.

'You've come a long way fast to wind a horse.'

The tall man had checked that the coffee pot was empty. Now he tipped out the used grounds on to the dirty plate and put in fresh. He added water and set the pot on the stove beside the pan.

'You really care?' he asked as he sat down at the table and used a forearm to clear a space in front of him.

'Just makin' conversation,' Hochman said defensively. 'Runnin' this place I don't get much chance to talk to folks.'

'Not your day, feller,' the tall man told him. 'I never talk unless I got something to say. And there's nothing else I want from you.'

'Okay!' Hochman said, and swallowed hard as he tore his gaze away from the cold stare of the tall man.

Outside, the buzzards squabbled for a few more minutes over their prize, then lifted into flight, bellies heavy with fresh horsemeat. Inside, the pan and the pot began to boil. The two men breathed the fetid air. Hochman remained seated tensely on the bed while his unwelcome guest altered the small sounds disturbing the peace. He poured himself some coffee after first rinsing the mug in the pan of water. Then he set the pan on the table and glanced around the room like a man not expecting to find what he was looking for. He went out and, through the open doorway, Hochman saw him search through his saddlebags. He came up with a bar of soap and brought it back. Stooped over the table, he washed his hands and face, scrubbing at the dried sweat and grimed trail dust ingrained in his pores. Then he reached under the long hair at the back of his neck and drew an open razor from the pouch that was faintly contoured by his shirt. The steel blade glinted in the sunlight and Hochman realised that shaving was only a secondary purpose of the razor. For a man to carry it in such a way meant it had to be primarily a weapon.

There was no mirror in the room and the tall man didn't need one. He shaved blind, with fast expertise: long, firm strokes that cropped the stubble to nothing on his cheeks and jaw, to leave a drooping moustache along his upper lip. He used his neckerchief to wipe the razor dry and remove the excess lather from his face. In the vee of his open shirt collar, Hochman saw the thong, strung with coloured beads, which held the razor pouch in place at the nape of his neck. Now that the coffee had cooled, he began to drink it. He grimaced at the taste as he dug a hand into a pants pocket. He drew out some change, counted out ten cents and put the coins on the table.

'What's that for?' Hochman asked nervously.

'The coffee ain't good, but I'm a man who pays his way. I reckon the shaving water was free?'

The blue eyes made the comment a query and Hochman nodded. 'Sure, mister. And I wasn't plannin' to charge you for the coffee.'

'Didn't ask.'

Hochman swallowed hard. 'Anything you say, mister. I got to attend to the horses. The westbound makes a long haul to here. Needs a fresh team to get to Monksville.'

'Ain't stopping you.'

'Thanks,' Hochman said, and as he hauled himself to his feet, he wondered why he had expressed gratitude. But, when he was outside in the bright sunlight, beyond the aura of death which seemed to emanate from the tall man, he certainly felt grateful for the fact. Then he shrugged off the mood and headed for the stable, cursing himself for a fool.

Inside the way station, the man who made the old-timer so nervous took the makings from a shirt pocket and rolled a cigarette. He lit it from the stove and returned to the chair at the table. From his hip pocket he took a slender billfold and extracted an envelope. The telegraph billhead inside was creased and dirty from much travel and a great deal of handling. But the message printed upon it was still legible and the burnished features of the man became set in a hard mask of anguish and evil as he read the words yet again.

'Hey, what the hell you doing here?'

The tall man had not got past the name and address prefacing the telegraph: EDGE SILVER LODE HOTEL VIRGINIA CITY NEVADA. But he knew the rest as well as he knew the name by which he was called and the address where he had been staying when the message was delivered.

'Please, I just slept in the stable, that's all. I didn't mean no harm.'

Edge carefully refolded the telegraph, slid it into the envelope and put this back into the billfold. The question had been yelled by the old-timer who ran the way station. The reply was pitched higher: a younger voice, sounding like the speaker was little more than a boy. A very frightened one. There were no windows looking out from the back of the way station and Edge had to pull open the door to look across at the stable on the other side of a fenced yard.

He saw the old-timer backing out of the stable doorway. Beyond him, advancing from the deep shadows within the stable, was a youngster of about eighteen. Medium height, medium build and moderately handsome. Brown hair, and brown eyes staring out of a wan face. Dressed in torn and stained dungarees over a check shirt. His hat hung down his back from the neckcord looped around his throat.

'You was tryin' to steal a horse!' Hochman challenged.

The youngster spotted Edge and stared, swallowing hard. Hochman glanced over his shoulder and now his weak eyes behind the lenses looked at the tall half-breed in the manner of one seeking an ally.

'He was tryin' to steal a horse, mister.'

Edge took the cigarette from the corner of his mouth and dropped it into the dust. He heeled out the red ambers. 'Not mine, feller,' he said evenly. 'So it's not my problem.'

The old-timer swung his head around to stare back at the youngster. 'What you doin' here, kid?' he demanded. 'How'd you get here?'

They were both nervy as they faced each other across

a gap of ten feet, the old-timer out in the sunlight and the boy in the shadows of the stable doorway.

'Look,' the kid gulped. 'I'm in trouble. Back in Monksville they say I did somethin' I didn't. I had to get out fast. My horse threw a shoe and split a hoof last night. I walked ten miles to get here. I really need a horse bad, mister. And I ain't got no money to buy one.'

Hochman pointed a filthy hand past the boy into the stable. 'Wouldn't matter if you did have, son. Ain't none of them animals for sale. And even if they was, I wouldn't sell one to no outlaw. So you get on your way. And if the law officers come lookin' for you, I'll tell them you was here.'

'You bastard!' the boy yelled, his eyes bright with sudden anger and a threat of tears. 'I didn't do what they said I did.'

He pushed a hand into a side pocket of the dungarees and snatched out a Remington .44. With a gun in his hand, the anger calmed and the tears retreated. His arm was rock steady as he aimed the gun at Hochman.

'Don't be crazy!' the old-timer croaked.

'Not your problem, mister?' the boy shouted at Edge, flicking his gaze towards the half-breed, then returning his attention to Hochman.

'Ain't my horses,' Edge replied.

'But he's on the run from the law!' the old-timer croaked. 'He's said so.'

'That ain't my problem, either,' Edge answered. 'Long time since I wore a badge.'

'That's not the point!' Hochman yelled angrily.

'Make it a habit to mind my own business, feller.' His expression became pensive and he looked at the youngster. 'One thing?'

'Yeah, mister?'

'How many horses in there?'

'Eight.'

Edge looked at Hochman. 'How many to make up a fresh team?'

'Four. But that ain't the point, neither. This kid is – '

Hochman curtailed his protest as it became obvious Edge was not listening to him. He whirled to face the stable again and saw that the youngster had turned to go back inside. For long moments he stayed where he was. Then he lurched forward in a staggering run. The youngster heard the thudding footfalls and spun around. He had started to replace the Remington in his pocket, easing the hammer back to the rest as he did so. The sight of the old man running towards him re-kindled his old fear. A pitchfork was leaning against the wall just inside the doorway and Hochman snatched it up. As the wickedly pointed tines were aimed at the youngster, fear became panic.

His thumb, greased by sweat, slipped off the hammer and the gun exploded as he jerked it from his pocket. The bullet burst clear of the denim from which the dungarees were made and drilled a hole through the toecap of his right boot. Blood bubbled up through the punctured leather. He screamed and fell sideways. It saved his life, for at the moment he started to fall, Hochman hurled the pitchfork. The humble tool, become a deadly weapon, flashed past the youngster's canting body and thudded into the front of a stall. The long handle quivered with the force of the impact.

His right leg paralysed by the foot wound, the youngster had corkscrewed to the hay-and-dung littered floor. He landed on his back and his head swung one way and then the other. First he saw the wicked tines sunk into the wood. The horror this generated swamped his pain and, as he turned his face and the gun towards Hochman, yet another emotion altered the set of his features and expression in his eyes. He was gripped by an all-consuming rage.

Hochman, shocked by the violence of his own action, had pulled up short the moment the pitchfork left his grasp. Now his eyes begged for mercy and he thrust his arms out in front of him, hands splayed.

'Please, son?' he pleaded, the words shooting the mess of tobacco out of his mouth. 'I went wild. You take a horse, I'll lose my job. This is my life. I won't have nothin'.'

But the youngster wasn't listening. His rage remained high, but controlled. With slow deliberation, he cocked the

Remington, then gripped the butt with both hands to steady his aim. Hochman's words dried up as he stared into the gun muzzle. He clasped his hands at his chest, in prayer. Then he dropped hard to his knees, his body jolting with the impact. When he closed his eyes, the youngster lowered the aim of the gun and squeezed the trigger.

As after the first shot and scream, the stage line horses snorted and scraped at the ground in their stalls. But there was no panic among the well-schooled animals. Hochman toppled to the side and rolled on to his back. From the rear doorway of the way station, Edge saw the bright bloodstains spreading over the old-timer's thigh before Hochman's hands clawed at the bubbling hole. His scream faded into a low moaning sound.

'He tried to kill me!' the youngster snarled incredulously as he sat up. He stared frantically from the pain-wracked form of Hochman to Edge, who was leaning casually against the doorframe.

From far off to the south – beyond the rear of the stable – came the just discernible beating of many hooves against sun-baked ground. Edge didn't answer. Merely cocked his head, listening to the approach of the horsemen. The youngster was too incensed to be aware of anything outside the bounds of his own hatred and rage, directed at the injured old-timer.

He tried to stand up, but putting weight on his holed foot exploded pain through him again. It served to stoke his emotions and he dragged himself with awkward haste across the littered floor. Just as agony fired his feelings, so the desire for revenge augmented his strength. He hauled himself upright by clawing at the stall. The Remington slipped from his sweating hand. An attempt to retrieve it almost toppled him and he abandoned the gun. Then, favouring his right leg, he jerked the tines of the pitchfork out of the wood. Using the implement as a crutch, he hobbled across the stable towards the moaning Hochman.

The horsemen were much closer now, the beat of galloping hooves seeming to visibly vibrate the foul air trapped inside the stable. But Hochman, awash in a sea of pain, and the youngster, gripped by a thirst for vengeance, did not hear the swelling sound.

The old-timer did sense new danger, and snapped open his eyes. He stared up through the smeared lenses of his spectacles and his moans of pain became a scream of terror. The youngster towered over him, standing on his one good leg. His hands were high above his head, fisted around the pitchfork's pole. As he drove the tines downwards, he lost his balance and the falling weight of his body added to the power of the killing thrust. Petrified by fear, Hochman remained inert except for the quivering of his lips as he continued to vent the scream.

The four pointed curves of rusted metal plunged into the old-timer's belly and sank deep. His scream rose to a crescendo as the skin was punctured. He was dead, and silent, a part of a second later when the tines went clear through him and jolted to a halt against the hard-packed ground beneath him. Rings of blood broadened their staining of the check shirt around each plugged wound.

The youngster released his hold on the pitchfork and flopped across the head of the dead man. He rolled off, on to his back.

'He tried to kill me!' he gasped, couldn't hear his own words and raised his voice to a roar: 'The old bastard tried to kill me!'

Then he realised why he had to shout and his rage became terror. Only now, as the horsemen reached the way station and skidded their mounts to dust-billowing halts, did the youngster become aware of them. He powered himself on to his belly and started to crawl back to the stall where he had dropped the Remington.

Edge knew he wouldn't make it. The eight-man posse, only one of whom was wearing a badge, had stopped their rearing, snorting horses beyond the yard fence. All leapt from the saddles with guns drawn and scrambled over the fence. Two slowed as they approached Edge, covering him with Winchesters. The others, led by the sheriff, ran towards the stable doorway.

'Hold it, Andrews!' the lawman snarled as he skidded to a halt.

But the youngster kept on going, scrabbling at the ground with his hands and pushing hard with his good foot as the injured one dragged. The sheriff pumped a shell into the breech of his Winchester and squeezed the trigger. Dust showered down from the roof where the bullet smashed into a beam. The youngster froze.

'That's better!' the sheriff muttered and everyone heard the soft-spoken words. For now, with everyone motionless, only the sounds of heavy breathing disturbed the silence.

'Something you fellers ought to know,' Edge said evenly, flicking his ice-cold stare between the tense faces of the two men who covered him. 'I got an aversion to having guns pointed at me. I give people one warning. The second time it happens. I do more than talk about it.'

'Clem, get the iron!' the sheriff ordered. 'Ben, tie up the prisoner.'

The two designated men tore their horrified gazes away from the gruesome sight of Hochman's body pinned to the stable floor and advanced to do the lawman's bidding. Then, when he was certain the situation was under control, the sheriff turned slowly to look across the yard at Edge. By accident or design, he allowed the Winchester barrel to sink towards the ground. He was a man of middle years, clean-shaven, bright-eyed and neatly groomed under the sweat and dust of a hard ride. He was about six feet tall and solidly-built. He tried to look impassive, but his full lips were slightly twisted with the image of the dead man fresh in his mind.

'What part did you play in this, mister?' he demanded, indicating the scene in the stable with a backwards gesture of his head.

'They weren't playing,' the half-breed answered flatly.

'You were a witness?'

Edge pointed a long, brown finger at the two men covering him. 'Tell them to aim the rifles someplace else.'

The bright eyes of the lawman raked Edge from head to toe and recognised the latent menace in the man. But he also realised the half-breed wanted no part of the trouble unless he was forced into it. He nodded to his men and the Winchesters dropped their aim towards the dirt.

'Obliged,' Edge said with a sigh. 'The young guy was trying to steal a horse. The old-timer tried to stop him. The young guy didn't cotton to that. The young guy shot himself in the foot. He didn't cotton to that, either. He got mad and killed the old-timer.'

'And what did you do while all this was going on?' the lawman asked as the trembling and sobbing Andrews was dragged out of the stable.

'Watched.'

The sheriff expressed contempt. 'Just watched? Didn't you try to stop it?'

Edge spat into the dust outside the doorway and dug into his shirt pocket for the makings. 'Was none of my business.'

The fervent buzzing of flies feeding on the congealing blood of Dan Hochman provided a low-key background to the youngster's diminishing sobs. Every other man in the posse stared at Edge in the same manner as the sheriff.

'Your kind make me sick to my stomach!' the lawman snarled at the half-breed.

Edge ran his tongue along the gummed side of the cigarette paper. His eyes – no more than narrow glints of blue between the lids – shifted their stare from the lawman to the youngster. 'Don't know if it'll help, feller,' he replied as he struck a match on the doorframe. 'But why don't you take Andrews?'

The sheriff grimaced and swung towards the two men who had dragged the youngster from the stable by the shoulder straps of his dungarees. Andrews' hands were lashed together at his back by his own bootlaces. 'Load him on a horse.' He indicated two other men with his free hand. 'Take that thing out of the body and load both. We'll need the pitchfork for evidence.'

The men did as instructed. Those in charge of the prisoner handled him roughly. Those handling the dead man did their chore gingerly. Everyone pointedly avoided looking at Edge as the half-breed calmly smoked his cigarette. Then, all the posse except for the lawman remounted their horses on the far side of the fence.

'You'll be needed in Monksville for the trial,' the sheriff rasped. 'Got a horse?'

'Out on the trail. Dead.'

'How?'

'I shot him. His unlucky day. Your lucky one. Waiting for the ten o'clock stage into Monksville. If you hold the trial while I'm in town, you've got nothing to worry about.'

The sheriff scowled. 'Your kind always worry me, mister.'

'Obliged for your concern.'

Now the lawman spat. 'What's your name, mister?'

'Edge.' He looked hard at the sheriff, but the name produced no reaction and he had already shown he was not good at concealing his emotions.

'What Edge?'

'Just Edge.'

'Okay. I'm Bill Harman. Be in my office when the stage reaches Monksville. Right next door to the depot. We can get a conviction without your evidence, but I'm telling you to be on that stage.'

'I told you already, sheriff. I intend to be on the stage.'

Harman nodded, spun around and strode across the yard. The lanky, square-faced man named Clem led the sheriff's horse close to the fence and Harman swung into the saddle from the top rail.

'You're trusting him to come in on his own, Bill?' the short, paunchy, round-faced Ben asked.

'Why the hell shouldn't he?' Harman growled. 'What's he got to lose except a little time telling the judge what he saw here?'

He glared at Edge and received a nod of agreement.

'I'll be there, sheriff.'

'And you'll stay to watch the hanging, I'm betting,' Harman responded with heavy contempt, his words springing a gasp of despair from the prisoner.

Then Harman raised a hand high in the air and thrust it forward. He and the rest of the posse slammed their heels against the flanks of their mounts and the horses lunged back on to the trail and were turned to head south. The group went out of sight behind the bulk of the stable. When they reappeared, they were enveloped in the dust cloud raised by the pumping hooves. By the time Edge had smoked his cigarette the sound of the posse's departure had faded and a leaden silence was pressing down over the mountains which formed the eastern side of Death Valley.

Because he needed to get to Monksville and the stage would require a fresh team to take him there, the half-breed ambled across the yard and into the stable to feed and water the horses. The big, strong, well-cared-for animals eyed him balefully as he attended to their needs.

'Yeah, I know,' he rasped. 'But I got my own problems.'

One of the horses snorted, baring his yellow teeth.

'The old-timer shouldn't have pitched in,' Edge growled. 'His fault he got stuck with it.'

CHAPTER TWO

IT was the first syllable in the name of the town towards which he was headed that awoke a memory in Edge's mind as he re-entered the way station and stretched out on a bench in the public room. That, and the fact that the youngster with the lethal temper was destined to be hanged. For, way back in the April of 1864, it was in a monastery that he and six Union troopers under his command got their first period of rest after escaping execution in a Richmond prison.

They were still in Rebel-held territory, south east of the Confederate capital and a mile north of where the James River cut a long curve through the lush Virginia countryside on its way to the Atlantic Ocean. But they were more secure than they had been at any other time during the long, violent, and bloody War Between The States. For the high-walled monastery, in its idyllic pastoral setting at the foot of a grassland slope, had been thoroughly searched by Rebel soldiers only hours after the Union men blasted their way inside. The Confederates had failed to find the wanted escapees and had left. There was no reason for them to return and, since the monks were self-supporting, no need for anyone to venture outside further than the sloping meadow where the livestock grazed.

So, apart from ensuring that the neutral monks confined themselves to their religious and household pursuits, the seven Union men who had tried unsuccessfully to assassinate the Confederate President, Jefferson Davis, had nothing to do except rest and recuperate. But, because of the basic nature of some of the men and the aggression which war had instilled in others, this period of inactivity could not last for very long.

It endured until mid-July, the troopers becoming progressively more disenchanted with their inactivity as, unknown to them in the distant theatres of war, the fortunes of the Union and the Confederacy swung this way and that. The shoulder wound Captain Josiah C. Hedges had suffered on the run down the James River on a Rebel ironclad healed. So did the bullet hole in the arm of Corporal Hal Douglas. Both men, together with Sergeant Frank Forrest and Troopers Billy Seward, Bob Rhett, John Scott and Roger Bell, ate well and slept a great deal. They grew fit and filled out, replenishing their bodies and spirits after a long period of deprivation. The sun shone and their no longer haggard features became tanned. The battles at Jenkins Ferry, The Wilderness, New Market and Cold Harbor were fought, won, and lost. The Union laid seige to Petersburg, Virginia and, off the coast of France, sank the Rebel ship *Alabama*. A Confederate thrust reached the outskirts of Washington D.C. before it was repulsed. Then, on the day that the Union forces under Major-General A. J. Smith routed the Rebels in the Battle of Tupelo – July 15 – Hedges knew it was time to re-join the war.

It was a bright, warm day and he was sprawled out under the north-facing wall of the monastery, stripped to the waist and dozing. It was noon and the day was progressing much like any other since he had imposed his routine on the religious retreat. He, Scott and Bell were off-duty. Douglas and Seward were up on a wooden look-out platform in the north-west corner of the quadrangle, from which they could see all over the fertile basin of land in which the monastery was situated. Rhett and Forrest patrolled the cloisters and cells, the chapel and communal rooms to ensure that the monks did only what they were supposed to do. The men on duty wore monks' habits and cowls and were armed with Spencer rifles and Confederate Colts. The off-duty men carried only holstered revolvers – with the exception of Hedges who also had the razor in his neck pouch.

Bob Rhett triggered the incident that was destined to plunge the Union troopers back into the war. A tall, thin New Englander, Rhett was the one bad apple in the fighting unit composed of the seven men: bad in the sense that he was a gold-bricker and a coward. The fact that he was also a homosexual was immaterial, except when his preference caused trouble.

He saw the naked monk as he used the muzzle of his Spencer to push open the door of the bath-house in the south-east corner of the monastery. So far, he had undertaken his patrol duties of the morning with bored indifference. Not enjoying the aimless wandering along flagged corridors and through gloom-shrouded rooms, but accepting the dull routine as better than the terrifying prospect of returning to a battle zone.

Then, as the heavy door swung away from him, a lustful grin spread across his shallowly handsome face. The monk, who was in his early twenties – a little younger than Rhett – had just stepped from the tub and was stooped over, tipping the dirty water into a gutter. He had his naked back towards the doorway and the splash of water masked the sound of Rhett's advance into the room. It was a long room, but narrow: the excited New Englander reached the unsuspecting monk in three strides. He stood for a long moment, swallowing hard and licking his lips as he feasted his hungry eyes on the twin curves of firm, white flesh presented before him.

Then: 'Oh, brother, have you got what I want,' he rasped.

The monk dropped the tin bath-tub with a clang and whirled around. He was shocked to see the hooded head, then terrified as he glimpsed the rifle and realised he was faced by one of the Union soldiers. He gasped and took a step backwards. His bare foot sunk into the gutter and he tripped and fell heavily to the floor. Rhett laughed and sent the cowl down his back with a toss of his head.

'Please!' the young monk begged. 'Your officer has promised we will not be harmed if we co-operate.'

Rhett surveyed the youthful face with approval, then raked his glinting eyes down over the matted chest, rapidly rising and falling stomach and finally fixed his gaze on the hirsute tangle between the trembling thighs.

'That's what I want,' Rhett said softly, as he rested the Spencer on the bottom of the overturned bath-tub and began to work on the fastenings of the habit. 'Co-operation.

And it won't harm you. I'm the most gentle of partners.'

'It's bestial!' the monk shrieked. 'I have forsaken all pleasures of the flesh. Even before I joined the order I never – '

Rhett shrugged his shoulders and the habit slid off him. His thin torso was clothed only in an undervest. He took off his gunbelt and laid it across the rifle before starting to jerk the undergarment over his head.

'Don't knock it until you try it, sweetheart,' the New Englander urged throatily. He dropped the undervest on top of the habit and started on the fastenings of his pants. The front of them bulged in a more powerful show of lust than was displayed on his sweating face.

'Please!' the monk begged more fervently. 'Don't do this thing. It will be a most heinous violation of my vows.'

Rhett giggled as his belt slid free of the buckle. 'So what, sweetheart?' he challenged in a taunting tone. 'You're a religious man.' He made a circling motion with a finger. 'So do what the Good Book teaches you. Roll over, my handsome, strong friend. Turn the other cheeks.'

The monk, his entire body and all limbs trembling, started to comply with Rhett's demand. His lips moved in a silent prayer and these signs of terror served to heighten the pitch of the New Englander's excitement. For as a coward Rhett relished having a man at his mercy: and as a sexually aroused animal he anticipated meek submission with greater delight than having to commit rape.

But, a second later, his ecstatic excitement became icy terror. He crouched down to push off his pants and Long Johns and they snagged on his boots. The monk was getting to his feet, pressing himself against the rough stone wall. Rhett looked down at the disarray of clothing around his feet and delved his hands into it to jerk off his boots. The monk, his lips still moving in the frantic, silent prayer, lunged away from the wall. Rhett caught a glimpse of fast movement and snapped up his head. The lust drained from his eyes and his mouth gaped wide.

'No!' he screamed at the top of his voice, powering upright.

He should have thrown himself forward – towards the overturned bath-tub at which the monk was diving. But, from a swaggering bully, the New Englander switched to a craven coward. He tried to whirl and run. One of the monk's hands held the holster against the bath-tub as the other drew the Colt.

'Help!' Rhett shrieked as he half-turned and then was thrown to the flagged floor by the tangle of clothes around his feet. A high-pitched cry of pain exploded from him as his hip and shoulder slammed into the paving. 'Captain! Frank!' He rolled over on his back and stared with terror-filled eyes at the naked monk. The man was aiming the revolver at him, gripping it with both hands and with two fingers hooked around the trigger. Rhett's voice became a hoarse whisper as he forced out the words from his constricted throat. 'Hey, I was kiddin', monk. Foolin' around, you know? I only come for a bath, that's all.' As fear contorted his face, so the throbbing physical effect of his lust shrivelled.

'Bob, you couldn't come no way with a little thing like that,' a harsh voice rasped from the open doorway of the bath house.

The monk was still praying. His eyes flicked up and saw another habit-garbed form in the doorway, aiming a Spencer rifle at him. The cowl was hung down the man's back to reveal the mean-eyed, sour-mouthed features of Frank Forrest.

'God, forgive me,' the monk said aloud, and jerked both fingers against the trigger.

There was no movement and no report.

Rhett gasped back the nausea that had risen into his throat. Then a high giggle burst from his trembling lips.

The monk stared in horror at the gun.

'He didn't cock the friggin' thing!' the New Englander yelled.

Forrest showed his tobacco-stained teeth in a grin of evil enjoyment. 'These religious nuts ain't like you, Bob,' the sergeant rasped. 'They got their minds on higher things than cock.'

He squeezed the trigger of the Spencer. He was aiming it casually from the hip, confident of his skill. The report resounded within the bare stone walls of the bath house, swamping the muted scream vented from the monk's mouth. He took the .30 calibre bullet in the centre of his heart. The impact slammed him back against the wall, an arc of spraying crimson gushing from the hole in his chest. Then he crumpled to the floor and fell forward, bridging the gutter. The blood continued to flow, emptying down the waste hole in the corner of the room.

Outside in the sunlit quadrangle voices were raised and running footsteps sounded. Men raced into the corridor leading to the bath house and the sound effects of excited confusion were amplified by echo.

The Colt had dropped from the hands of the dead man and Forrest reached it in four long strides. He steadied the gun with a boot on the barrel as he stooped down to cock the hammer.

Men skidded to a halt in the doorway and Forrest looked into their shocked faces gravely. Rhett forced himself to sit up and struggled to hoist his Long Johns and pants.

'Let us through, you bastards!' a voice yelled.

Violent movement among the monks opened up a gap and John Scott burst into the room, followed by Roger Bell. Both were heavy eyed from many hours of sleep. They looked from the fully-clothed, rifle-toting Forrest to the hurriedly dressing Rhett and then at the naked body of the monk.

'What we miss, Frank?' Scott asked excitedly.

There was another disturbance out in the corridor and Hedges forced a way into the room. The narrow strips of his eyes took in the scene at a glance and the impassiveness of his expression hardened as he stared at the sergeant. The elderly father abbot moved into the space at the doorway left by Hedges. He muttered a blessing for the dead man and the other monks chanted in response. Then silence descended upon the murky room, disturbed only by the small sounds of Rhett clothing his body.

'Well, sergeant?' the Captain demanded.

The officer and the non-com stared coldly at each other, eyes locked together. For the first time since the unit of Union cavalry men had arrived at the monastery, the question of command rose to the surface. It was not a new question. Ever since Hedges had been joined by these six troopers at the opening of the Shenandoah Valley Campaign he had only been able to retain command by proving himself to be smarter, harder and tougher than Forrest.

The sergeant was the oldest member of the group and had entered the war with a long experience of bounty-hunting in the south-west and Mexico behind him. Hedges was an Iowa farm boy who had to learn to kill. The others, with the exception of Rhett, had had to learn the same lessons. And they learned fast and well. But none of them possessed the quality of leadership. Only Hedges and Forrest could claim this. It had been apparent from the start that the other five were prepared to follow either the Captain or the sergeant. And rank did not matter, for they regarded the military chain of command and the same lack of respect as every other aspect of army discipline and order. They were soldiers only because they had once been issued with uniforms and the army paid them. In essence they were born killers granted legal carte blanche to indulge their pleasure. And this made them into the ideal fighting unit for the kind of war they had been forced to fight – excepting only that they were inclined to resent Hedges for his officer ranking and give their allegiance to Forrest. Thus, the Captain was only able to retain tenuous command over the men by constantly winning battles of wits and will against the sergeant.

Forrest rasped the back of a hand over the morning growth of stubble on his jaw. 'It was the monk or Rhett, sir,' he said and his tone and the use of the courtesy title were good signs. He shifted his boot behind the Colt and sent it skittering across the floor towards Hedges. 'Heard some yellin' in here and come runnin'. The monk had the iron aimed at Rhett. So I blasted the monk before he could blast Rhett.'

Hedges swung his hard-eyed stare towards the New Englander, who was standing up now and pulling the undervest over his head. 'How'd he get your gun, trooper?' he growled.

Rhett was trapped by the cold, ice-blue eyes under the hooded lids and he swallowed hard. 'Gee, Captain. It's kinda hot today. A guy sweats a lot in these habits. I figured to take a bath, that's all. I thought these guys didn't go for shootin' and stuff like that.'

'They don't go for stuff like that!' Scott put in lightly.

Bell laughed.

Rhett looked away from Hedges to treat the two troopers to a withering glare. Then he swallowed again. 'So I just started to undress, sir. Next thing I knew the monk had grabbed my gun and was pointin' at me. Lucky that Fra . . . Sergeant Forrest happened to be outside.'

'A brother would not do such a thing unless provoked!' the father abbot said angrily.

'Shut up!' Hedges barked at him, then fixed Rhett with another hard-eyed stare. 'You lie the way you do everything else, trooper,' he snarled. 'Lousy.'

Rhett draped the habit around his shoulders, pulled the cowl over his head and picked up the Spencer and gunbelt from the overturned bath-tub. Hedges crouched down, scooped up the Confederate Colt and arched it underarm at Rhett. The New Englander caught it. The silence became leaden in the bath house again.

Hedges half turned and looked about him. At the monks crowded in the doorway, whose horror was giving way to anger. At Rhett, who avoided meeting the appraisal with his eyes by concentrating on refitting the gunbelt around his waist. At Scott and Bell, who were gazing at the slumped body with unconcealed excitement. Finally, at Forrest, who responded with a quizzical look in his eyes. Then the mean-faced non-com exhibited his ability to read the way Hedges' mind worked.

'Time to call a halt to the furlough, Captain? Rhett lit the fuse and the whole joint is liable to explode. Them and us.'

Hedges parted his thin lips to show his teeth in an icy smile. 'I reckon, sergeant,' he agreed and captured Rhett's fearful gaze. 'No matter how often you take a bath, trooper, you'll still stink!'

'Hey, Frank!'

All attention was focused upon a slit window high in the wall. Billy Seward was stretched out flat on the roof, hanging over the edge to peer upside-down into the bath house. The good eating and abundance of rest he had experienced over the past few months had fattened his features. He looked more deceptively baby-faced than ever. In fact, he was probably the most vicious killer among the group of Union troopers.

'Get back to your post, soldier!' Forrest snarled. 'And you and Douglas be ready to pull out any time!'

'Yeah, man!' Seward yelled in high excitement. 'What brought this on?'

'Gonna be a blow up, Billy,' John Scott called to the trooper on the roof.

'The monks are burnin',' Bell added.

'Beat it, I said!' Forrest yelled.

Seward's grinning face disappeared from the window. Scott and Bell grinned at each other.

'Bob wanted a bang,' Scott said.

Bell laughed. 'And he didn't even make a little poof.'

Because hard experience had proved that survival could depend upon it, Edge had learned to be a light sleeper. Thus, when the stage rounded a distant outcrop of rock and broadcast the sound of its approach ahead of it, he came awake to instant awareness and automatically fisted a hand around his revolver butt. But then he recognised the intrusion of sound for what it was and gathered up his gear. He stepped out on to the porch to wait for the stage.

It came fast, trailing a long cloud of dust from under its rolling wheel rims and the pumping hooves of lathered horses. The dust rose higher and was thicker as the ageing driver hauled on the reins and brake lever to skid the swaying Concord and its bulging-eyed team to a halt. Edge cracked his eyes against the irritating dust and stepped out of the shadowed porchway. The driver and the much younger guard eyed the tall, heavily-laden half-breed anxiously. The latter tightened his grip on the Winchester resting across his lap.

'Don't do it, feller,' Edge warned softly.

'Do what?' the driver asked as he licked dust off his lips.

Edge sensed eyes watching him from within the stage. Nervous eyes. 'Not you,' he said. 'The other one. Don't point that gun at me.'

The guard laughed nervously. 'Gee, mister. You startled me, stepping out into the light like that. Where's Dan Hochman?'

'Who's he?'

'Old guy who manages the way station,' the driver explained.

Edge approached the stage. 'He's gone to Monksville.'

'He's got no right!' the driver growled.

'He had no choice,' Edge answered, pulling open the door. 'Sheriff took him in. Morning to you.'

This last was addressed to the elderly woman and two middle-aged men comprising the stage's passengers to the Funeral Mountains Way Station.

'Good morning, young man,' the woman said brightly. She was about seventy and had lived too long to be afraid of anything.

Both the men wore the suits and hats and carried the black valises of drummers. They glanced at each other, reached a tacit agreement and confined their response to curt nods. The stage rocked as Edge settled into a corner seat and dumped his gear on the floor, the saddle resting in such a way that the stock of the Winchester jutted conveniently up from the boot. There was a lesser creaking of the springs as the driver and guard shifted their weight down to the ground. The driver appeared at the open door.

'What you mean, the sheriff took him in?' he wanted to know. 'What'd Hochman do?'

'His job, and got a pitchfork in his belly for taking the trouble.'

The old lady gasped. The drummers paled beneath their newly-acquired tans.

'Hochman's dead?' the driver said and gulped as he turned to look at the guard. 'Dan Hochman's dead?'

Edge didn't reply.

'How'd it happen?' the guard wanted to know. 'Who killed him?'

Edge sighed, and took out his billfold. 'For you folks, the same as me,' he said softly. 'None of our business. Mine is in Monksville.' He flicked his cold-eyed gaze between the driver and the guard. 'Yours is to get me there.' He took a ten dollar bill from the fold and thrust it across the stage. 'Be obliged if you'd attend to yours.'

The driver took the bill like an automaton, still staggered by the news of Hochman's death. He gulped again. 'You can't just leave it in the air like that, mister,' he protested.

Edge had taken out the telegraph and unfolded it. He read it: EDGE SILVER LODE HOTEL VIRGINIA CITY NEVADA IF YOU WANT TO FIND OUT SOMETHING ABOUT YOUR WIFE COME TO MONKSVILLE CALIFORNIA NANCY.

The half-breed's eyes narrowed still further as he replaced the telegraph in the envelope, the envelope in the billfold and the billfold in his hip pocket. 'Reckon I can,' he said to end the long pause. 'Same as I can hitch a new team and drive this rig into town. In which case I'll have my money back.'

Anger flared across the time-lined face. 'Ain't no one but me drives this stage, mister!' he retorted.

'So do it, feller,' the half-breed urged softly. 'Fresh horses are out back. Fed and watered.'

The driver seemed poised to continue the argument, but the guard tugged at his arm.

'Come on, Mort,' the younger man urged. 'Don't mess with him. We'll get the story in Monksville.'

Mort hesitated, then allowing himself to be drawn away from the stage door. He went around to the stable yard while the guard unhitched the old team. The drummers stared hard at the unchanging view across Death Valley, as if they were fascinated by it. The old lady watched Edge with more genuine interest.

'There's a dead horse back along the trail, young man,' she said at length, as the team were taken from the traces and led to the rear of the way station.

'I know, ma'am,' the half-breed replied.

She made a sound of annoyance with her tongue against her dentures. 'There is no call to be so close-mouthed, young man,' she challenged.

Edge pursed his lips, then parted them in a smile that did not reach his eyes. 'Tell you something, ma'am.'

'What?' She leaned forward, her interest heightening. The drummers were suddenly bored with the view beyond the windows.

'If you don't stop flapping yours, I'll have to close it for you.'

The drummer seated immediately across the aisle from Edge leapt to his feet, flabby face spread with the scarlet of high anger. 'That's no way to speak to a lady!' he challenged.

The half-breed shot out a foot and the saddle canted fast. The stock of the Winchester slammed into the drummer's crotch. The man grunted with pain, reached down to its source, and bent forward. Edge streaked a hand to the back of his neck, delving beneath the hair. The hand came away fisted around wooden grip of the razor. His other hand swept forward, knocking off the drummer's derby and grabbing a bunch of the greasy brown hair beneath. Still seated himself, he jerked the man's head down further and brought across the razor. He rested the blade under the fear-flared nostrils of the drummer.

'Oh, my God!' the other drummer groaned, pressing himself hard into the corner.

'Ladies got manners,' Edge rasped, and pressed the razor just enough to erupt three tiny trickles of blood from the sides and centre of the man's nostrils. 'My Ma and Pa always taught me manners was keeping your nose out of other folks' business. How d'you feel about that, feller?'

The drummer swallowed hard. 'Sure, mister. Sure thing.'

Edge removed the razor and slid it back into the neck pouch. Then he put the heel of his hand against the drummer's forehead, relaxed his grip on the hair and shoved. The drummer thudded painfully back into his seat.

'Oh dear, I was just interested, that's all,' the old lady croaked, her throat arid.

The stage rocked as the new team was hitched up to the traces.

'Curiosity's killed more than mangy cats, ma'am,' the half-breed told her, wriggling into a more comfortable position on the hard-padded seat. He tipped his hat forward over his eyes. But one hand rested close to the butt of his holstered Colt. 'It's wasted a few old bitches, too.'

The driver came to the side of the stage to close the door. He saw the injured drummer holding his crotch with one hand while the other pressed a handkerchief to his bloodied nose. 'What's going on?' he demanded gruffly.

He eyed the lady, who was flushed from the insult, the rigidly erect drummer sitting opposite her and the totally relaxed half-breed.

'A minor altercation on the subject of manners,' the uninjured salesman blurted out in a cultured accent.

'No problem,' Edge muttered from under the brim of his tilted hat. He stabbed a finger at the man seated opposite him. 'Until he brought sex into it. Let's move it, Mort.'

The driver hesitated, then decided that it would be safer not to get involved. He slammed the door, climbed up on to the high seat and took the reins. The guard remained at the way station and the driver shouted a promise to send out a relief from Monksville on the night stage. Then he flicked the reins and yelled at the team.

Although in an attitude of sleep, Edge remained fully awake as the stage creaked and juddered along the well-used trail striking south through the mountains. For a while, he thought about Beth: the way he had met her, the way he had married her, the brutally short life they had together, the way she had died. He didn't know much about her, but he had always considered he knew enough. Then the telegraph had reached him and proved he was wrong. He didn't know anyone named Nancy and had never heard of Monksville yet here he was, on the final stretch of the long journey to Monksville where Nancy would be.

What could she tell him about a dead woman that would make any difference to him? Nothing. For Edge was what he was to an extent that he could not be changed. Except by death. Then he would be dead and it wouldn't matter. But while he lived . . . Beth had begun to change him, with his willing consent. Then her death – and the harsh manner of it – had forced him back deeper than ever into the mould out of which she had tried to rescue him. His grief had been long and harrowing and when he was drained of this, he was also bereft of every other finer human feeling.

He had thought, at first, that he was merely repeating an earlier experience: becoming hard and bitter and vicious just as he did when he returned from the war to discover the dead and mutilated body of his brother. But this had proved not to be so. For, many violent years after he finished grieving for Jamie and the future he might have had, Beth had entered his life and rekindled the warmth of human emotions latent beneath the hard exterior shell.

Then he lost Beth, more tragically even than the way in which Jamie died. And, since that ghastly day when he found her maggot-infested, decomposing body, Edge had known that nobody and nothing could rescue him from what he had become. Except death.

'Monksville up ahead, folks!' the driver yelled from atop the rocking Concord. 'Be there in five minutes. Like always, right on the nose.'

Edge pulled up straighter in his seat and tipped his hat back squarely on to his head. He grinned when he saw the injured drummer put exploratory fingers against the congealed blood at his nostrils. 'Unfortunate choice of words,' he drawled, flexing his shoulder, arm and finger joints.

The drummer refused to meet the half-breed's gaze and made an excuse of snapping open his valise and peering inside. The old lady sniffed and the other salesman attempted a nervous smile. Edge looked out of the window and saw that the sun was threequarters of the way down its descending arc. Still harshly yellow and blazing a hot, dry heat that hung in a shimmering white haze around the foreshortened horizon on all sides. They were a lot lower now, racing fast through the red, brown and yellow hills at the southern tip of the Funeral Mountain range. No vegetation on either side of the trail, except for the cactus plants and the scattered patches of mesquite brush. But, as the trail curved to the east to skirt a broad, primeval crater scooped in the water-starved ground, the half-breed counted three trees growing amid the cluster of buildings that formed Monksville. The bell of a public clock began to toll mournfully. Mort spurted the team and the clatter of its hurtling progress was amplified between the façades of buildings facing each other across the street. Skidding wheels showered dust and galloping hooves kicked up pebbles. Then the stage had rounded a corner and Mort fought it to a rocking halt at one side of a square. The final, fifth, note of the striking clock diminished into the heat-hazed distance beyond the town.

'Dead on time again!' the driver yelled.

'And plain lucky all your passengers ain't dead, the way you drive!' a man growled angrily.

'My driving ain't never harmed nobody!' Mort retorted, swinging around in his seat to begin unstrapping the baggage from the rack.

'That is a matter of opinion, sir!' the old lady said airily as the Monksville agent for the stage line helped her down on to the sidewalk. She massaged her rump.

Both drummers remained firmly in their seats, as if afraid they would raise the half-breed's anger again if they tried to take precedence over him. Gear held easily in both arms, Edge stood on the step on the opposite side from the sidewalk and surveyed the town.

The three trees he had seen from the trail were all in the central square. Live oaks providing shade for the wooden benches set beneath them. The square was the business area of Monksville, fringed by the stage line depot, law office, courthouse, four stores, a saloon, church and livery stable. A street entered the square on the north and the south side and each was flanked with small, neat houses in patches of small, neat gardens. Only desert plants grew in the gardens. The legal and commercial buildings were all constructed of red brick and rough stone. The houses were frame. Everything looked clean and new, except for a large proportion of the citizens. Strolling ladies with parasols and men lounging on the benches under the shady trees had a neat and well-scrubbed appearance, but old: a lot of them senile.

Few showed more than idle curiosity in the stage and its passengers.

'You're the one they call Edge?'

The half-breed turned on the step and peered over the roof of the stage. The speaker was one of the few people on the square who did not have a time-lined skin and age-stooped body. She was standing in the doorway of the stage depot, a tall, slender redhead with an excitingly curved figure outlined by a tight-fitting white blouse: high-necked and nipped in at the waist by the belt of a flared black skirt. Her hair was held in a bun at the back of her head. Her face should have been pretty, but there was a certain hardness in her green eyes and the way her mouthline was formed. She was about twenty-five.

Edge stepped down from the stage and ambled around the back and up on to the sidewalk. He knew he had the kind of harshly-formed features that either attracted or revolted women. The green eyes appraised him with cold interest.

'Only woman in Monksville who'd ask that would be named Nancy,' he said.

The minor stir caused by the arrival of the stage was over. The old lady had been met by another of similar age and was being escorted towards the street on the south side of the square. The driver had gone into the depot to learn the story of Dan Hochman's killing. One of the drummers – he who had provoked Edge's anger – was heading for the saloon. The other salesman entered the pharmacy, which was the largest store in town. Edge and the woman were alone on the stretch of sidewalk outside the depot.

She nodded. 'Nancy Harman, Edge.'

She was twenty years younger than the sheriff and the family resemblance was faded.

'Related to the man with the badge?'

'She's my sister!'

The lawman snarled the answer from behind Edge. The half-breed did not turn his body. Just his head, and saw the solidly-built Harman standing outside the doorway of his office. His attitude was tense and he was aiming a Winchester from the hip. The boards of the sidewalk creaked as the woman backed away. Edge turned his head again, ignoring her and raking his eyes to the corner of the stage depot. Two more Winchesters were aimed at him from there, tightly-held by two men he recognised from the posse which had trailed Andrews to the way station. He didn't know their names, but the familiar set of their features caused his hooded eyes to glint with the menace of ice-cold anger. Nancy Harman backed into the corner of the stage depot doorway, out of the danger of crossfire. The chests of of the two men facing Edge rose and fell and evening sunlight glittered on the deputy's badges now pinned to their shirt fronts.

'You heard the warning I gave you back at the way station,' Edge said evenly.

The parked stage blocked his view of a large part of the square. But he heard the shuffle of hurrying feet as the strollers and loungers withdrew to a safe distance.

One of the deputies licked his lips and the other gulped. Nancy peered fearfully out of the depot doorway. In the deeper shadow behind her the agent was looking shocked. Mort was showing excited interest.

'You're a wanted man, Edge!' the lawman snarled. 'Give yourself up peaceful.'

'Wanted for what?'

'Murder.'

The half-breed's narrowed eyes flicked constantly between the two deputies. He was sweating from the heat, but they were sweating a great deal more. He parted his thin lips in a tight smile. 'Which one, sheriff?'

'Elliot Thombs.'

'In Kansas, a long time ago. Old hat and out of your jurisdiction, feller.'

'Not of the man who's comin' to get you.'

'If he moves fast, I may still be here,' Edge said evenly.

Then he lunged for the depot doorway. It was a risk, but a calculated one. For he had decided Harman was the kind of man who would hesitate a vital fraction of a second before shooting another in the back. The deputies were tied up in knots by tension and if they opened fire, it would be in panic. Either Harman or he could be unlucky enough to be hit by a wild shot. Maybe neither.

Nancy screamed with alarm and staggered backwards, crashing into Mort and the agent. Edge had to take two diagonal strides across the sidewalk to gain the cover of the doorway. He didn't go for his gun, using both hands to hold his gear high in front of his head and torso. His prediction about the reaction of the lawmen proved to be right.

All three were frozen for an instant by the unexpected lunge from a man who had apppeared to be standing so casually. Then Harman threw the stock of his rifle up to his shoulder. The two deputies fired simultaneously from the hip. One of the bullets struck the horn of the half-breed's saddle and ricochetted through the doorway ahead of him. Its trajectory changed from level flight into a decline. Nancy Harman had sat down hard between Mort and the agent, and kept from sprawling out full-length by grabbing at the legs of the startled men. The act killed her. The bullet, no longer rifling, turned end-over-end and smashed a great hole through her top lip. A man screamed – not in the depot.

Nancy went on to her back now, a great stream of blood gushing from her mouth. The major wound was in the roof of her mouth and only some of the blood escaped. Most of it drained down her throat and swamped her lungs. That in her mutilated mouth became frothy with bubbles of escaping air.

'Women!' Edge growled as he dropped his gear and drew the Winchester from the saddle boot, working the lever action. 'Just can't stop running off at the mouth.'

He lunged forward again, crashing between the two stage company men and leaping the body of the woman at which they were staring. There was a counter with a flap open and he raced through and up a stairway at the rear of the room. At the top was a square landing with doors leading off. He used the heel of a boot to smash open one and sprinted across a spartanly-furnished bedroom. The window was open and he paused for a moment, narrowed eyes raking the square. It was deserted. But he could see the pale blobs of watchers' faces behind windows. There had been no more shooting. But the deputies were moving now.

'Bill Harman's dead!' a woman shrieked. 'The sheriff's been shot!'

Edge listened to the slow footfalls of the deputies on the sidewalk beneath the canopy outside the window. He lifted his right foot to rest it across the windowsill. Then he poised himself.

'Come outta there, Edge!' one of the lawmen yelled.

There was a tense pause. Then Mort ended it with a hoarse whisper.

'He's gone for the roof, Eddy!'

Hunching his shoulders to make the gap, Edge launched himself through the window. He powered into a turn in mid-air as he cleared the canopy, and bent his knees as he landed sure-footed on the roof of the parked stage. One of the deputies was crouched by the window of the depot while the other was starting towards the doorway. They were not aware of the half-breed until his boots thudded against the wooden roof. Then they started to whirl, snapping their rifles around. Edge took the one at the window first, blasting a shell into the side of his head. The force of the impact was enough to drive his blood-spewing body crashing through the window. The Winchester swung as the action was pumped. The second deputy was drilled through the chest, a half inch above where his badge was pinned. His rifle exploded as he was flung back against the wall. The bullet splintered wood chips from the driver's seat of the stage and whined high into the air.

Edge did a complete turn, raking the Winchester at the same pace his slitted eyes surveyed his surroundings. The square was as deserted as before. But now three bodies oozed blood to stain the sidewalk; the two men Edge had killed and the sheriff. Harman was curled up in a heap outside the doorway of his office. He had taken the wild shot low down on the right side of his chest. From the vast amount of blood he had lost, through the chest and mouth, it had taken a few seconds for the punctured lung to kill him.

'Anyone else got business with me?' he yelled.

'I sure enough ain't,' Mort rasped from the shaded interior of the stage depot.

Edge gripped the roof-rack rail and vaulted down to the sidewalk. He looked levelly in through the open doorway. 'You already talked out of turn once, Mort,' he warned. 'Best you keep your mouth closed in future, uh?'

Mort nodded emphatically, pressing his lips tightly together. Edge canted the rifle across his shoulder, reached in through the doorway and hefted his gear one-handed. As he turned, a priest emerged from the hardware store on the far side of the law office. He hurried to where Harman lay and squatted beside the corpse. He crossed himself, his fleshy face solemn.

'Sir!' he called sharply as Edge stepped down from the sidewalk behind the stage.

The half-breed halted and eyed the man coldly.

'If you wish to ask forgiveness for the tragedy you have brought to this town, my church is across the square. Next door to the saloon.'

Edge glanced at the two buildings beyond the live oaks and then showed the priest a mirthless grin. 'That arrangement's real handy, feller,' he allowed. 'For folks that thirst after righteousness.'

CHAPTER THREE

ALTHOUGH Hedges had intended that he and his men should remain at the monastery for as long as it was safe to do so, he had started preparations to leave from the first day they arrived. This had entailed ordering the monks to make seven sets of top clothes for the Union men, to replace the motley selection of soiled uniforms and tattered civilian garb they had worn when they entered the monastery.

Thus when, at nightfall, the troopers gathered inside the big main gate of the monastery, they were garbed in pants and jackets fashioned from monastic habits and shirts made from bed linen. The clothes were cut to different styles and had been rapidly aged by hard wear to conceal their newness. Hedges, Forrest and Douglas had gunbelts and holsters. The others carried their Confederate Colts in the waistbands of their pants. Each man had a Spencer rifle and pockets bulging with shells.

The atmosphere in the monastery during the afternoon had been tense and there had been no off-duty periods for the troopers. While the look-out platform continued to be manned, the other five troopers kept the monks herded into the main chapel. Then, as darkness fell, each intruder by turn went to dress and arm himself.

Now the entire population of the monastery was out in the quadrangle, partly brightly illuminated by the three-quarter moon hanging low in the eastern sky and partly in deep shadow. The monks were closely grouped in front of the cloisters on the far side from the gate. Despite their religious training and faith, the anger they felt towards the soldiers was like a tangible force suspended in the warm night air separating the large and small bodies of men.

'We just gonna leave them like that?' Scott whispered. 'They'll be out and runnin' for the nearest Reb camp soon as we're outta sight.'

'We oughta lock 'em up someplace,' Douglas growled.

'I say blast 'em!' Seward rasped, and grinned in eager anticipation.

The monks could not hear the exchange except as an incomprehensible murmuring. But as they sensed their fate was being discussed their mood changed from low-keyed anger to silent anxiety.

Forrest drove the troopers into silence with a sweeping, mean look at each of them in turn.

'Father abbot!' Hedges called.

'Yes?' the aged, senior man answered.

'Come here!'

'What for?' His voice was abruptly tremulous.

'Sergeant,' the Captain barked.

Forrest eyed the troopers again and this time he showed his teeth in a humourless grin. 'Single file and take aim,' he ordered. His voice rang out between the high, stone walls. He lowered it to a whisper. 'If more than one of 'em comes at us, blast the whole bunch.'

'You reckon heaven can handle the sudden rush?' Rhett asked as the men formed the line and Forrest joined on the end.

'Answer enough for you?' Hedges yelled.

The father abbot took only a moment to make up his mind, and had to shrug off grasping hands as he broke from the group of monks. His face against the cowl was white with fear, but his stride was strong and he held his head high. He stopped two feet in front of Hedges and the Captain ignored him. He stepped to the side.

'We're taking your head man,' he announced. Then had to shout louder as a murmur of protest rose from the monks. 'Save the words for your prayers!' he roared. 'He'll be with us for two hours. Then he'll get turned loose. He's an old man and he'll be bushed, so it'll take him longer than two hours to get back here.'

'How do we know you'll release the father abbot in two hours?' one of the monks called.

Hedges' teeth gleamed in the moonlight. 'You don't, feller. Maybe we'll hang on to him for six hours. Only one thing you can be sure of. Any Johnnie Rebs tag us, the old guy enters the promised land. Some things I lie about, others I don't.'

'May God have mercy on your soul!' a monk wailed from the rear of the group.

'Obliged for the thought,' Hedges growled, and turned towards his men, who were still lined up in the attitude of an execution squad. 'Sergeant, open the gate. Corporal, you take care of our insurance.'

'I like the Captain's policy,' Douglas said with a grin, swinging his Spencer towards the father abbot as Forrest began to shoot the bolts on the gate.

'Just keep that guy well covered,' Rhett put in, and giggled.

'Move out,' Hedges ordered. 'But not like soldiers. Which ought to be easy for you guys.'

At the order to move, the men had automatically shouldered their rifles and swung into an about-face. But, with the supplementary command, they became a loose-knit, slouching group. Hedges raked his eyes around the inside of the monastery for the final time, looked fleetingly at the monks, then followed his men and slammed the gate closed behind him. Footfalls thudded against the turfed centre of the quadrangle and, as the Union troopers moved off into the moonlight-bathed country, striking north, they sensed many pairs of watching eyes following their progress. But only their elderly prisoner looked back. Just the once, for Douglas enjoyed power when he had it, and he jabbed the muzzle of his rifle hard into the small of the monk's back.

Soon, with everyone matching the fast pace set by Hedges, the group were up out of the basin in which the monastery was sited. For a few moments they were clearly silhouetted against the cloudless, star-sprinkled night sky. Then they were gone from the view of the frightened-eyed monks.

Hedges kept the pace fast across the gentle, verdant hills of eastern central Virginia. They crossed a broad belt of farmland, but the local population had been decimated by the South's hunger for fighting men. For every one thriving farmstead they came upon, there were several which had been abandoned – derelict buildings standing amid fields and meadows choked by weeds. Initially, the glow in the night sky that marked the position of Richmond had been slightly ahead of them, far to the west. Then they drew level with it and finally put it behind them.

They had been walking, without seeing anybody, for more than three hours when they emerged from a large stand of timber and saw the stud farm on the river bank. Of the eight men, only the elderly father abbot felt the strain of the trek, and he sank gratefully to the ground when Hedges raised a hand signal to halt. Forrest moved from the rear of the group to the front and stood beside the Captain, adding his experienced gaze to the survey of the terrain ahead.

'If I'd enjoyed walkin', I'd have joined the infantry, Captain,' he muttered with a grin. 'That looks nice.'

'Still calling the shots right?' Hedges asked wryly.

He had been aware of the soft-voiced gripes of the men as he had led them on the cross-country hike. Growls of protest that became more bitter with each farmstead they skirted instead of attacking. Forrest had not silenced the men, but neither had he voiced his own feelings. Now the tough sergeant broadened his grin.

'I know you, sir,' he said. 'Just as well as you know me. We hate each other's guts but we got this understandin' about that, ain't we? The war can't last for ever and we gotta stomp the Rebs into the ground before we settle our own differences.'

'Unless I steer us wrong before that?' Hedges replied, still examining the buildings and corrals of the stud farm which began five hundred yards away.

Both men conversed in normal tones, for the enmity between them and the agreement to bring this to the logical, deadly conclusion at a later date was common knowledge among the troopers.

'Sure thing, Captain. But you ain't done that yet. I figured you was as ready as the rest of us to get out of that house of God freaks back there. And I reckoned, like you, that wasn't one of them farms had enough of the kind of mounts we need. So you're still callin' it right, sir.' He jerked his

Spencer towards the stud farm. 'And that, like I said, looks real nice.'

Hedges nodded, then showed Forrest his own brand of mirthless grin. 'Then let's go and mess it up a little, Sergeant. Straight on down then, split back and front of the house.'

'What about the holy man, Captain?' Douglas asked.

Despite his ability to remain cool in most circumstances, Hedges could feel as exhilarated as his men at the prospect of killing in the heat of battle. This showed now in the narrowing of his glinting eyes and the way the firming up of his mouth-line stretched the skin taut over his high cheekbones. The aged monk recognised the evil intent in the face and altered his posture from a squat to an attitude of prayer.

'He ain't done a thing to us,' Hedges rasped. 'But we owe him. Stick with him, Corporal. When it's over down there, turn him loose and come running.'

Disappointment was displayed on Douglas's face and he stayed his hand as he was about to pump a shell into the breech of the Spencer. Then Hedges and Forrest swung around and set off towards the stud farm. The others followed close behind, beginning to sweat with the anticipation of killing again after such a long lay-off.

'He don't look like he has,' Douglas snarled softly at the father abbot. 'But that sonofabitchin' Captain's got a soft streak in him.'

'There is good in all men, my son,' the monk said, unable to conceal the relief he felt.

'You reckon?' Douglas said sourly and spat against the trunk of a tree.

The old man stared at the departing soldiers, moving in a crouching run across a stretch of grassland, then clambering over the fence of an empty corral: intent upon slaughter and probably not remembering the cause in the name of which they committed their legal atrocities.

'Difficult as it is to have such faith in these troubled times, I firmly believe it, my son.'

Douglas checked that the attacking group was far out of earshot of muted sound from the timber. Then he stared malevolently at the back of the father abbot as the old man got painfully up from his kneeling posture.

'You believe in crap like that, gotta be somethin' wrong with your head, holy man!' he snarled, and allowed the Spencer to slide through his hands.

He had the rifle gripped by the barrel when the old man sensed the menace in the quiet wood and began to turn. The Spencer made a slight hissing sound as it arched through the summer night air. The father abbot tried to duck out of its path, but the aged joints were slow to respond to the dictates of his panicked brain. The lower angle of the heavy wooden stock crashed into the back of his head, powered by every angry ounce of the trooper's restored strength. Just a tiny gasp – little more than an expelled breath – was uttered as the old man toppled to the ground like a felled tree. In the foliage-filtered moonlight, Douglas was able to see the slick, dark-coloured stain spreading over the back of the cowl.

He reversed the rifle and used the foresight to draw aside the blood-soaked cowl. The anger drained out of him and a sneer of enjoyment spread across his face as he saw the white of a shattered skullbone gleaming amid the ooze of blood and brain matter.

'I was right,' he muttered and the sneer became a grin and then expanded into a giggle. 'You got a hole in it.' Then he had to cover his mouth with his hand to mute the uncontrollable laughing fit that gripped him. 'Now you really are a holy man,' he gasped.

He leaned against a tree, his stomach painfully knotted by the effort to contain the near-hysterical joy he felt. None of the Union troopers lived by bread alone. Because of the way in which war had twisted their minds and unleashed the latent evil which lurks deep in all men, they were no longer whole unless they were able to satisfy their lust for killing. First Forrest, now Douglas. Two of the seven who needed to kill as well as to eat and drink in order to exist had ended their long fast.

Advancing on the peaceful stud farm, Forrest anticipated his second helping of violence in one day while the others relished their keen anticipation of the animalistic pleasures which they had been denied for so long.

Hedges had detailed his plan as they approached the objective and it was launched with stealthy silence. First they checked that the stud farm was as flourishing as it looked from its well-preserved buildings and neatly kept corrals. They saw four brood mares in one stable, a half dozen colts in another and ten stallions in the third. None of the doors were locked and the stallions raised no noise when Rhett entered their stable. He held up four fingers to indicate to the men at the doorway that there were that many saddles and bridles strung from wall pegs.

As the New Englander began to cut a coil of rope into lengths, the other troopers split into two groups. Forrest, Seward and Scott remained behind the single-storey frame house while Hedges and Bell went around to the front. All the windows were dark, until Hedges used the stock of his Spencer to bang on the panelled wood door. Then, in quick succession, lamps were lit in three parts of the house. Heavy drape curtains filtered the light which was shed outside.

'Pa, there's someone at the door!' a man yelled.

'I ain't deaf!' an older voice responded with a note of sourness.

'Shall I get the door, Mr Weller.' This was another voice. Also a man.

'I ain't helpless, either!'

'Sounds like a grouch,' Bell rasped, levelling his rifle at the centre of the door.

Hedges' teeth glinted in the moonlight. 'And he don't even know who we are yet.'

Two of the lighted windows were at the back of the house. Forrest went to the rear door and Seward and Scott closed in on a window each. Hedges eyed the lighted window two removed from the front door, on the right. But the drapes remained firmly in place. He could hear a man cursing softly, then a strip of light appeared at the foot of the door. The man's tread was lighter than his mood.

Seward heard a fourth voice behind the window at which he was poised.

'Who can it be at this time of night, John?' Soft, frightened and female.

Seward licked his lips and drew in a deep breath. The lack of opportunity to indulge his psychopathic enjoyment of killing had not been the sole shortcoming of the long stay at the monastery. Like the rest of the men, he had not set eyes on a woman the whole time he was there. A new brand of excitement stirred inside him.

'How the hell do I know, Marsha?' the man sharing the room with her growled.

'I don't like it, John. Go with father in case –'

'Okay,' the man sighed and his feet hit the floor hard.

'Atta boy,' Seward murmured.

At the front of the house, Hedges gestured for Bell to go to the window. The excited trooper went, striding long and silently along the cement-floored porch.

'Who's there?' the obvious head of the household called in the familiar disgruntled tone.

Hedges placed him immediately on the other side of the door and he adjusted the aim of the Spencer. 'Got some news for you, Mr Weller,' he answered solemnly.

'Who is it?' John wanted to know. 'Is it them? They're early!'

'Shuddup!' This to John. Then: 'What you mean?'

'Bad news. We're always bad news.'

There was a gasp, probably not from the old man. When he spoke, there was no fear in his voice. 'I don't know who you are, mister, but you ought to know I got me a shotgun pointed as the door. Two barrels.'

'Obliged for the information,' Hedges replied.

Then he went down into a crouch and squeezed the trigger of the rifle. He aimed from the shoulder, the muzzle no more than six inches from the panelling of the door. The first bullet penetrated the centre of the wood at about waist level. He pumped the action, swung the rifle to the right and fired. Pumped again and raked it left to blast a third hole in the door. The much louder report of both loads of a double-barrelled shotgun being discharged swamped the crack of the third rifle shot. A gaping hole appeared high up in the door. Blackened shards of wood showered the crouching Hedges as the buckshot sprayed through the air.

Windows had been smashed immediately his first shot had signalled the attack. As he powered upright, he glanced to his right and saw Bell ducking in through the window he had shattered with his Spencer stock.

'John!' a woman screamed.

Hedges's hooded eyes peered through the black-edged hole exploded by the shotgun and took in the lamplit scene in an instant.

'Marsha!'

An old man in a night shirt was sprawled on his back. He had been hit twice by bullets on a rising trajectory. One had taken him in the shoulder and the other had gone in under his jaw and burrowed a course through the roof of his mouth into his brain. One dead hand was still wrapped around the frame of the shotgun which had exploded its dual load as he fell backwards.

A younger man dressed only in a sheet draped over his shoulders, had whirled and started to run back down the hallway. The height of the hole in the door made a rifle shot awkward and Hedges drew his Colt. The woman in the back room vented a scream of terror.

'John!'

'Marsha!'

'That can go on for ever,' Hedges muttered, drew a bead on the back of the running man and fired.

The slug took him high up, left of centre, and he pitched forward, the blood-stained sheet dropping from him to reveal his nakedness underneath.

Seward risked cutting himself to ribbons. When he heard the signal shot, he took three backward steps, then lunged forward, rifle held crosswise as he protected his face with his forearms. He smashed headfirst through the window and had the luck of the reckless. He sustained just one deep cut on the back of his hand as he hit the carpeted floor and Marsha shrieked her first plea.

He rolled over on to his back, raising the injured hand to his mouth to suck at the spurting blood. Then he sat up and his eyes widened with heightening lust, for in taking the single sheet to cover himself, John had left his wife with nothing to hide her own nudity. She was about thirty, an unpretty brunette, but with a well-developed body that looked like paradise to the long-denied Seward.

She screamed for her husband again as the youngster picked himself up off the glass-littered floor. John's second frantic response was followed by the revolver shot and thud of his body pitching to the floor. Seward dropped his hand and parted his blood-dripping lips to show a broad grin.

'Sounds like he ain't gonna make it, honey,' he said, allowing the rifle to drop to the floor. Then he shot out a hand to fix a clawing grip on her shoulder as she attempted to roll away. 'Looks like I am.'

She screamed and he lunged on to the bed, smashing a folded knee into her stomach. She vomited with pain and terror.

Forrest blasted the lock on the back door and crashed it open with a shoulder. He charged across the dark kitchen and threw wide another door. It opened in time for him to see John go full-length to the floor in the broad hallway. Bell ran into view from an archway to one side of the front door and the rapport which the men had developed over the long years of fighting side-by-side proved itself again. They sensed the other's presence before they saw each other, yet did not even flinch. They both looked at Hedges' face framed in the shot-gun-blasted hole at the top of the door.

'Whatever happened to Southern hospitality, you reckon?' the Captain asked lightly.

A man in his early twenties yanked open a door at the side of the hallway and lurched out. He was dressed in Long Johns. A bullet from Scott's Spencer cracked out of the room in his wake gouging a bloody rut across his upper arm. He turned towards the back of the house and saw the grinning Forrest. He screamed, pulled up short and whirled around. Bell and Hedges surveyed him from that direction with the same brand of evil good humour. Scott lumbered into the doorway of the room from which the man had escaped. The man stared into the open doorway of the room across the hall and saw Seward fumbling open the front of his pants as he held the struggling, vomiting woman a prisoner beneath him.

'Why?' he screamed at the top of his voice, the veins standing out like blue ropes on his neck.

He snapped his head in all four directions again, his wide eyes pleading. Four rifles and a revolver cracked, belching more blue gunsmoke to strengthen the taint already thick in the hot air.

'Because you were there,' Hedges said softly as the body corkscrewed to the floor, gushing thick crimson from the wounds in its naked torso.

'Billy's got a dame!' John Scott yelled furiously as the man crumpled in front of him and gave him a clear view into the bedroom opposite. Then he stared at Forrest. 'God-damit, Frank, Billy's got himself a friggin' woman!'

Bell sprinted forward, curving around the body of the old man at the door and leaping that of the naked John. But Scott lunged into the room first. Then Forrest. Bell was third to swell the audience for the rape that was being enacted on the big double bed.

Seward yanked himself out of the front of his open pants and grinned at the men crowded in the doorway. Then he used his knees to force wide the woman's legs and thrust himself into her. Marsha gasped with pain, and the final violation of her body drained her weakening will to resist further.

'*Yiiipppeeee!*' Seward yelled in wild delight as he began to drive his pent-up lust into the wooden unresponsive body of the woman beneath him.

'Come on, Billy, quit hoggin' that stuff!' Bell urged.

Scott didn't trust himself to speak: simply matched his heavy breathing to the cadence of the rapist's thrusting strokes.

Forrest watched the cruel act for long moments, experiencing arousal and struggling to quell it. In that time, more gunfire sounded from the front of the house as Hedges blasted at the lock and bolts on the door. As the door crashed open and the Captain's footfalls thudded in the hallway, the Sergeant advanced into the room. He reached the head of the bed as Hedges barged in between the two troopers on the threshold. Seward had his passion-crimson face buried in the woman's neck as he clawed at the mounds of her breasts flattened under his heaving chest. Marsha stared up at Forrest, her eyes imploring help while her vomit-run lips moved in silent pleading.

'Yes,' she managed to utter as Forrest drew the Colt from his holster.

'She likes it!' Seward moaned.

Hedges skidded to a halt halfway across the room as he saw what the Sergeant intended.

Forrest cocked the revolver, rested the muzzle against the soft flesh beneath Marsha's ear and squeezed the trigger. The gun was so angled that the bullet went up into her head, burrowed through her brain and burst clear of the top of her skull. Blood and grey ooze splashed around the hole in the bed headboard.

Seward yelled in terror and leapt off the abruptly still body. He hit the floor in a crouch and straightened up with a jerk, eyes bulging with insane rage as he stared at Forrest.

'You bastard!' he screamed. 'You blew her friggin' brains out!'

Forrest had slid the Colt back in the holster and now he aimed the Spencer at the crazed youngster's exposed genitals. 'Yours are hangin' out, kid,' he rasped. 'That weren't the kind of ride we come here to get.'

There was a tense period of stretched seconds when Seward seemed on the point of going for the Colt jutting from his waistband. Then, as his erection shrivelled, his rage subsided. A weak grin spread across his face, which was speckled with signs of the woman's nausea.

'That was some bang we give her, Frank,' he said, his tone ingratiating. He began to fasten the front of his pants.

Forrest dropped the aim of the Spencer and winked at Seward. 'She was crazy for it, Billy. Blew her mind.'

'Sweet Jesus, what a waste,' Scott sighed, raking his disappointed gaze over the naked curves and hollows of the corpse.

'What you do it for, Sarge?' Bell groaned.

''Cause he knew the Captain wouldn't go for it, that's why!' Scott rasped .

Forrest whirled, bringing up the rifle again. Scott saw the killer glint in the non-com's eyes and took a backward step. He came up hard against the wall. Hedges had no time to level his own Spencer. He simply stepped into the line of fire – facing the Sergeant. But it was to Scott he spoke as locked stares with Forrest.

'You're a stupid sonofabitch, trooper!' he said, his voice ice-cold. 'Forrest wanted to screw her worse than any of you.'

'So why – ?' Bell started.

'He's got to be first at everything,' Hedges cut in.

Now it was Forrest's turn to bring his killer rage under control. It took him less time than Seward. Just a second before he flicked his wrist to cant the rifle across his shoulder as he parted his lips to show his tobacco-stained teeth.

'Like I said, Captain, we know each other real good.'

'Aw shit, Billy, why didn't you wait?' Bell groaned.

Seward shrugged. 'You were all kinda busy shootin' up everythin' else around the house.'

'Hey, you guys comin'?' Rhett yelled from the corral immediately at the rear of the house.

Seward took a final look at the dead Marsha and spat as he stooped to pick up his rifle. 'No friggin' chance,' he muttered as Hedges turned to head for the door.

Forrest broadened his grin and draped an arm around Seward's shoulders, steering him in the wake of Scott and Bell. 'Tell you what, Billy,' he said. 'I'll give Bob the word you couldn't finish what you started. He'll give you a hand.'

There were a dozen customers in the saloon. Apart from the drummer with the bloodied nose who was at the bar, they were all seated at tables. Again with the exception of the salesman, they were all elderly – not one under sixty and some in their eighties. A few of them were breathing heavily and had crimson complexions from the strain of hurrying back to their tables after watching from windows and batswing doors. They avoided looking at the tall half-breed until he had passed them, dumped his gear on the floor and hooked a boot over the brass-rail at the foot of the bar.

His position, at the end of a direct line from the entrance, placed him six feet away from the drummer. 'Relax, feller,' he said evenly. 'We finished our business together.'

The salesman was rigid and he stiff-armed his shot-glass of whiskey to his lips. He sank it at a gulp and the liquor seemed to lubricate his joints. He nodded curtly. 'I'm sure glad of that, Mr Edge.'

The bartender had been talking to the drummer. They were about the same, mid-thirties age, but the bartender was tall and thin as opposed to the short build and broad girth of the drummer.

'Beer,' the half-breed requested.

The two pumps were immediately in front of him. The bartender approached them cautiously and his hands shook as he drew a glassful of the foamed, pale amber beer.

'Obliged,' Edge said, glanced at the price list pinned above the shelves behind the bar and dropped two nickels beside the glass. He swallowed half the drink at one go and nodded his appreciation of the relief it gave his dust-dry throat. 'Lot of old people in Monksville,' he said.

'You stick around, lot of us won't get no older, young feller,' a man at one of the tables growled.

Edge had addressed the question to the bartender, who had started to wash glasses that gleamed from recent polishing. Now he turned and leaned his back against the top of the bar. The direction in which everyone was looking pinpointed the man who had spoken. A man of about seventy, with a lot of silver grey hair atop a healthy-looking face out of which light brown eyes twinkled. Well-dressed in a city-style suit but with a white Stetson resting on the table beside a half-empty bottle of rye and a completely empty shot glass. He had mottled hands with fingers ringed by ornate jewellery. A gold watch chain arched across the front of his brightly-checked vest.

He was alone at his table.

Edge pursed his lips and wiped a line of clinging froth

off the top one.

'That a criticism or a comment, old-timer?' he asked evenly.

'Maybe a prediction?' the well-dressed man replied and poured himself another drink. His hand was rock steady, for he and Edge were the only unafraid men in the saloon. Everyone else was tense and expectant of the worst. 'Bill Harman was a good lawman.'

'I shot the deputies, I did not shoot the sheriff,' Edge reminded.

The old-timer sipped his rye. 'Does that matter?'

Edge grinned. 'Just want the record to be right.'

'You get the needle real fast, mister.'

'And I'm real sharp, ain't I, feller?'

The man nodded. 'Can't argue with that.' He sighed, finished his drink and stood up. He looked around the saloon. 'You men on the Town Council, come on over to the law office with me. We got us a new appointment to make.'

Five of the men stood up, none of them looking happy, and followed the silvery grey haired one out into the square. The light beyond the batswings was tinged red by the setting sun. Edge swung around towards the bar again and finished the remainder of his beer. He banged the glass on the counter top and nodded to the bartender for a refill.

'He the big white chief around Monksville?' he asked.

The man was still highly nervous and had trouble getting his vocal chords to work. But once he had started, he seemed reluctant to stop. 'That's Mr Scott Gerstenberg. He's the mayor. Him and the councillors got the job of trying to elect a new sheriff now Bill Harman's dead. Won't be easy. Harman had enough trouble swearing in a couple of temporary deputies.'

He put the fresh beer down and clawed the price into his apron pocket.

'Maybe the mayor predicted how temporary they would be,' Edge suggested wryly.

'Weren't on account of you, mister,' the bartender hurried to reply. 'Leastways, that's not what Bill Harman said. He reckoned as how Melody Devine's brothers were heading for town to give the Andrews boy what they reckon's due to him.'

Edge blinked. 'Melody Devine, for Chrissake?' he muttered. Then: 'What he do to her?'

He sensed a new mood emanating from the old men left in the saloon and glanced over his shoulder. They were hanging excitedly on the bartender's words.

'He had his way with her,' the bartender replied, dropping his voice. 'Against her will, you know what I mean?'

Edge nodded. 'Like a lot of other folks in this place, I can imagine.'

'Melody runs the drugstore across the square. Busiest store in town, on account of Monksville being a place so many old people have come to retire to. Old people get aches and pains, you know what I mean?'

Edge nodded absently, losing interest now that he knew as much as he needed to know about the situation in Monksville. But the bartender was one of those kind who could best control his emotions by constant talking.

'So she hired Jeff Andrews when he come riding through a few months back. Now, there's been stories about what went on between them two after the store closed nights. But ain't no one knows for sure. Don't matter now, though, 'cause there ain't gonna be no trial. All that matters is that Melody screamed rape and straight after he took it on the lam, she headed out for the Devine Ranch down south.'

Edge had been drinking his beer steadily. Now he set down the empty glass but made no motion for it to be filled a third time. The bartender showed him a shrug.

'With no one like Bill Harman around to protect the prisoner. Andrews ain't gonna be alive to stand trial. The Devine boys are real tough characters.'

'But you're tougher than ten of their kind, mister.'

Edge had lifted his gear when the voice of Gerstenberg spoke from behind him. He turned and saw the mayor halted halfway through the batswings. The faces of some of the town councillors looked over the doors. They still were not happy. The mayor wore an expression of calm expectation.

'You offering me a job, feller?' Edge asked.

'A temporary one.'

'Only kind I ever take.'

Expectation blossomed into a smile. 'Then you'll wear the badge?'

'Thousand dollars a day and – '

'You're crazy!' the mayor cut in, the smile fading as his brown eyes became as hard as stained marble.

' – I do it my own way,' Edge finished.

'No deal.'

The half-breed started towards the doorway. The councillors backed away, but Gerstenberg held his position until the last moment. He let the doors swing back into place so that Edge had to push through them to reach the sidewalk outside. Now, only the trailing half-sphere of the red sun showed above the ridges of the Panamint Mountains, visible in the far distance after the heat shimmer had been wiped from the horizon. A hint of the desert's night coldness was refreshing in the darkening air.

'Hey, Scott, they're comin'!' a man called, his tone reedy and anxious.

All eyes swung towards the roof of the courthouse. A man was crouched up there, clinging to a chimney. He was staring down into the square, but his free hand was pointing towards the south.

The mayor became apprehensive for the first time. 'All right!' he said suddenly, and glared around at his councillors, challenging them to contradict him. Then he fixed his hard stare on Edge's impassive features. 'A thousand. For one day. Circuit judge will be here tomorrow.'

The half-breed stepped down from the sidewalk, transferring all his gear to one arm. He held up the index and middle finger of his free hand.

'I said the circuit judge will be here – '

'Grand, not days,' Edge interrupted.

Anger turned Gerstenberg's features a violent scarlet. He tried to speak, but all that emerged was a string of strangled sounds. Spittle ran down his jaw.

'I just found out how badly you need me, feller,' the half-breed drawled as hoofbeats pounded against the fast-cooling air. 'I add it up to two grand bad.'

'Ain't no man worth that kinda money, Scott,' one of the councillors rasped as the sound of the approaching riders swelled.

They were in sight of the men on the square now – three of them galloping flat out along the south trail towards Monksville.

'Damn right!' the mayor snarled.

There was a rocking chair to one side of the saloon entrance. Edge dropped into it and rested his gear at the side, Winchester stock angled up within easy reach. He nodded his easy acceptance of the opinions.

'We've all got our problems. Mine ain't here yet.' He tipped his hat forward over his forehead and his narrowed eyes glinted more brightly out of the deep shadow. He began to rock the chair, very gently.

Gerstenberg looked desperately along the street and out on the trail. The riders were close enough now to be discernible as two men with a woman between them. He made a sound of disgust and dug a hand into a pocket of his well-cut jacket. He snatched out the badge taken from the corpse of Bill Harman and dropped it into Edge's lap.

'Fifteen hundred!' he growled. 'Not a cent more.'

Edge didn't move. The councillors did, hurrying to get off the square and into the cover of the saloon. The hoofbeats were very loud now, amplified by resounding off the façades of the buildings flanking the street.

'Will you do it?' the mayor asked and his anger and anxiety was mixed with a note of pleading now.

'Get lost, feller,' Edge said flatly. It could have been a refusal or a piece of advice.

Gerstenberg swallowed hard, then pushed through the batswing doors to enter the saloon. The trio rode into the square, hauling on the reins of their horses to slow the animals and angle them across to the law office. The body of Harman had been taken away: likewise those of his two deputies from in front of the stage line depot. The stage was still where it had halted, the team standing quietly in the traces. The newcomers flicked cursory glances at Edge then ignored him. Edge watched them carefully from under the tilted-forward brim of his hat. He saw a beautiful, statuesque blonde woman of about thirty who looked more than able to take care of herself in any trouble involving a youngster of Andrews' years and build. And two beefy men in their late thirties – high, wide and handsome. But the basically well-formed features of the whole family were contorted by the hatred in their hearts.

'Sheriff!' one of the Devine brothers yelled as all three horses were halted behind the stage, facing the law office. 'We come for the runt who dishonoured Melody!'

'Send him out here and he's the only one gets hurt,' the second brother shouted in the same tone, inviting no argument.

Edge set the chair to rocking harder and its motion caused the sidewalk planking to creak. The brothers turned in their saddles, dropping right hands to drape over their holstered Adams revolvers. The woman turned, too, but she wore no gun. Just a tight-fitting leather tunic and pants that showed off the strength and sexuality of her body and limbs. A low groaning sound began to come from the law office.

'Evening,' Edge said, and pushed his hat on to the top of his head.

The men glowered at him. Melody appraised him critically and he knew that she was one of the women who liked his looks.

'Where's Harman?' From the brother on the left.

'Dead.'

'How?' From the one on the right. 'He get Andrews?'

'Yeah.'

'You got any interest in him?' Melody asked.

'Ain't worth it.'

The woman smiled, showing a lot of perfectly matched, very white teeth. She had big grey eyes and the light of pleasure that entered them added to her basic beauty. 'Go and bring him out here, Lon,' she said.

The brother on the left slid smoothly from his saddle, hitched his horse to the rail and trod heavily across the sidewalk. Jeff Andrews' groans rose to a wail. The other brother dismounted and Melody unhooked a lariat from her saddle-horn.

'No, please don't!' Andrews shrieked.

The second brother hitched his horse and accepted the coil of rope. Everyone out on the square could sense many eyes watching from behind the surrounding windows.

'God have mercy!' Andrews screamed as a barred door was crashed open. 'Please, I didn't do any –'

A powerful fist smashed into flesh but there was no sound of a body falling. Footfalls hit the law office floor and then Lon Devine appeared in the doorway, the inert form of the accused rapist folded over his shoulder.

'Tie him to the stage wheel, Clayton,' Melody ordered. 'Then wake him up.'

Then she backed up her horse into the centre of the square and watched as her bidding was done. Her brothers sat the unconscious Andrews on the ground and Lon held him hard against the hub while Clayton took out a Bowie knife to cut three lengths from the lariat, then used them to lash the prisoner's arms and neck to wheel spokes. Satisfied with the progress so far, Melody stood in the stirrups and raked her gaze around the square. The clock on the front of the courthouse chimed the hour of six.

'You all know what that boy did to me!' she shouted. 'I was as helpless as he is now.'

Edge glanced at the batswings and saw several wan faces looking out over the top of the doors. 'That the way it happened?' he asked softly.

'Harman found her tied and gagged.'

Lon went back into the law office and Melody raked the square with her eyes again.

'She egged him on ever since she hired him,' someone whispered to Edge.

'He stands trial, all he gets is a prison sentence!' Melody shouted to her mostly unseen audience as Lon re-appeared, toting a bucket which slopped water over its brim. But there was still more than enough to shock Andrews into awareness when the contents were hurled into his face. 'And that's not enough!' the woman went on at the top of her voice. 'He had his satisfaction and now I demand mine.'

Since Edge was the only possible objector in clear view, she fixed her gaze on him.

'I don't want any interference!' she challenged.

Edge parted his lips in a cold grin. 'Look what's happening to the last guy who gave you any,' he replied.

Melody seated her well-sculptored rump back in the saddle and turned to look at the stage. Andrews, an ugly purple swelling on the side of his jaw, got the glaze out of his eyes and saw his predicament in sharp focus. He gaped his mouth wide to vent a scream.

'Geld him!' Melody commanded.

A series of gasps hissed from the saloon entrance. Andrews' scream was trapped in his terror-constricted throat. A woman in one of the stores emitted a choked cry. Clayton Devine went into a squat beside the helpless prisoner and stabbed the knife down the front of his pants, honed edge against the denim. He moved his hand outwards and downwards. Andrews wore nothing under his pants and, as the material parted from waistband to crotch, his hirsute genitals were exposed.

Melody had her back to Edge and he saw her become rigid with excitement. Andrews began to tremble. Tears started to merge with the runnels of water on his starkly white face and his breathing was suddenly short and fast. This pained gasping was all that disturbed the pregnant silence which gripped the town. Until Andrews' terror took control of his bodily functions and he urinated. Then the boy began to scream as he strained against his bonds. Lon Devine slid a black buck-skin glove on to his right hand and knelt down on the opposite side of the victim to his brother. The boy emptied his bladder and Lon, using his gloved hand, delicately lifted the obstructing length of flesh out of the way.

Andrews, his eyes seeming on the point of bulging from their sockets, started in ecstatic horror at the knife in Clayton's hand.

'Stop it, in God's name!' the man on the courthouse roof shrieked.

The knife descended.

'Two grand!' the mayor croaked.

The brothers hooked a heel over each of Andrews' legs, holding them apart. The knife dug into flesh. The victim's scream reached for the highest note and snapped. Blood spurted, then flowed as the knife was jerked to the side.

Edge had rocked back the chair as Gerstenberg blurted out the words. It tipped forward and the half-breed lunged erect, snatching the rifle from the boot and pumping the action. The Devine brothers heard the unmistakable clicking and scraping of metal against metal. The tin star fell off Edge's lap and landed right-side-up on the square. The brothers stared at Edge. Their sister whirled in the saddle and looked at the man, the fallen star and then back at the man.

The excitement on her beautiful face died, was replaced for an instant by rage, then triumph took over her features. 'You're too late to help him!' she shouted gleefully.

Edge had the Winchester levelled at the woman, aimed from the shoulder. But his slitted, glinting eyes flicked constantly between Lon and Clayton. 'Matter of priorities, lady,' he drawled. 'Self-help is what's important.'

Andrews was slumped back into silent unconsciousness. The blood, streaked with traces of white, continued to ooze from the mutilated flesh at the base of his stomach, darkening the stain on the sun-baked ground in the vee of his splayed legs.

'Arrest them sheriff!' Gerstenberg demanded from the saloon doorway. 'That boy's got to have medical treatment.'

'We already give him the treatment,' Lon Devine said wryly, eyes fixed on his brother's knife work.

'He was sure doctored,' Edge growled.

'You really are the new sheriff?' Melody said incredulously. 'Lot slower than Harman ever was.'

'Matter of shyness, lady.'

She laughed. 'You're shy?'

Edge spat across his forearm. 'Not me, lady. The mayor was shy: five hundred bucks.'

CHAPTER FOUR

'HEY, Hal, turn the holy guy loose and get on over here!' Forrest yelled.

Hedges was already mounted on a big grey stallion fitted with a saddle and leather bridle and reins. The Sergeant claimed a second saddled animal and barked the order across the meadow towards the timber as he swung astride the bay. Rhett had picked himself a fully-knitted mount and Seward beat Bell and Scott to the fourth one. The men cursed at having to ride bare backed, as the Corporal broke from the wood and began to run towards the corral.

Then a rifle shot exploded in the night and Bell's profanity became strident as the bullet cracked past his ear.

'Sweet Jesus!' Rhett moaned, and thudded his heels into the flanks of his horse.

The nervous thoroughbred reared and then lunged forward, galloping across the corral. The New Englander yelled in terror, but his cavalry training penetrated his emotions and he timed the leap over the fencing perfectly.

'Good old Bob!' Seward muttered, ducking low on his horse and swinging his head around as a volley of shots followed the opening report. 'Always ready for a jump.'

The other four had already pin-pointed the position from which the attack was coming. The river, with a trail along its bank, ran across the north boundary of the stud farm, then curved towards the south and entered a low-sided gorge. Muzzle flashes streaked the darkness in the mouth of the gorge and then the moving bulk of a group of riders was silhouetted against the moon-silvered surface of the river. They kept up the gunfire as they galloped, and lead smashed splinters off fencing and buildings and spurted divots of earth around the nervously-moving hooves of the stallions.

'You thinkin' what I'm thinkin' about Rhett, Captain?' Forrest yelled.

Hedges was looking at the approaching riders, narrowing the thousand-yard gap with every second. 'That for once he's had the right idea,' he rasped. 'Let's move.'

'What about Hal, Frank?' Scott shouted.

'You don't give a shit!' Forrest snarled back.

'I just asked.'

'Ride!'

Seward had already lunged his mount across the corral. Forrest was hard behind him, then Bell and Scott thudded in their heels. Hedges hesitated only a few moments. In that time, he estimated the strength of the attackers to be about twenty: and saw a small group become detached from the main body and veer away from the farm. His eyes raked ahead of them and he realised they had spotted Hal Douglas. The Corporal was still racing across the meadow in a flat-out sprint. He had no reserve of speed and he wasn't going to make it. But the men despatched to intercept him were holding their fire. Those closing on the farm were less sparing with their ammunition. Single shot and repeating rifle fire continued to crack across the corral.

'Captain!' he heard Douglas scream, and then he saw the Corporal trip and fall headlong to the ground, rifle hurtling from his grasp.

Hedges had caught hold of the rope bridle of the horse meant for Douglas. Now he released the spare animal and wheeled his own mount, heeling it towards the fence. 'Can't say it was good knowing you, Corporal!' he growled as he sent the big grey into a flying leap out of the corral.

His men, with Rhett far out ahead, were galloping in full retreat across pastureland bordering the river bank. It was flat, almost featureless country for as far as the eye could see in that direction. But on the north bank of the river the terrain offered a great deal more cover – rolling hills with many stands of timber. The river was the only obstacle: some forty feet wide and slow flowing. Hedges held his mount to a full gallop, still heading east and riding crouched in the saddle. Bullets snapped about him, and he sent no answering fire back towards his pursuers. Retreat was the right course to adopt, for they were a small force surprised by a much larger one. And, in full retreat, it was a futile exercise to waste effort and ammunition trying to pick off the enemy: for, with no opportunity to take aim, luck played too great a part. It was best to try to outrun those at the back, regroup in a stable situation and plan a strategy – to counter-attack or continue the retreat.

Hedges had come into the war with no formal military training for command. He had been commissioned, first as a lieutenant and then as a captain, because he had displayed basic common sense in every kind of situation. He had made decisions, after careful planning and on the spur of the moment, and followed them. Up until now they had always been the right decisions: and he made this one with the same calm confidence as all the others.

A glance over his shoulder showed that the large group of riders had reached the stud farm. The obstacle of the buildings and fences slowed their progress. The group who had captured Douglas were still in the meadow behind the farm, securing their prisoner. The main body of men was reduced still further as several leapt from their mounts to check out the house. Half – no more than ten men – swung around the front of the farm to maintain the chase, blasting lead across the pastureland.

Now Hedges fired for the first time since the route had started. Gripping the powerful stallion with his knees, he pumped the action of the Spencer, aimed the rifle into the air and squeezed the trigger. Then he took up the reins again and angled the horse towards the river. Every man ahead of him, with the exception of the terrified Rhett, snatched a glance over his shoulder at the sound of the single shot – much closer to them than the uneven volleys of fire sounding from the more distant pursuers. They saw the direction in which Hedges was riding and curved their own galloping mounts on to a parallel course. Rhett, clinging so low and tight to his horse he seemed to be as one with the animal, continued to be carried due east across the flat grassland.

And, for a while, he was the safest man in the Union unit. For he remained a fast-moving dark shadow against the darkness of the land, broadening the gap between himself and the enemy. Hedges, then Forrest, Seward, Scott and Bell plunged their mounts into the river. The change of direction had enabled the pursuers to draw closer. Then they were clearly defined targets – black against the moon-silvered backdrop of the river. And slow-moving as the horses lost their footing on the silted bed and had to swim.

Hedges was still separated from his men by more than sixty feet but made no attempt to close with them. For as long as they were crossing the river they were exposed to the fire of the horsemen behind them and every trooper in the water took the shortest course to the cover on the far bank – a straight line.

There was a brief interruption in the gunfire as the enemy slowed from the headlong gallop and awaited an order: whether to plunge into the water and give chase or to halt and send a concentrated fusillade towards the escapers.

The Union men were a quarter of the way across as their pursuers began to rein in their mounts. Hedges swung around in the saddle and drew his Colt: sent three rapid shots backwards for effect. Seward followed his example. Forrest used his rifle. One man on the bank screamed and pitched from the saddle of his skidding horse. With no stirrups or saddles, Scott and Bell could do no more than cling to their horses and curse the animals into greater speed.

An order was finally bellowed at the men on the bank and they leapt from their saddles as the horses halted. The Union men looked back yet again and at last glimpsed whom their pursuers were. In the direct moonlight, and the glow refracted from the surface of the river, they were able to make out the glinting buttons, badges of rank and unmistakable shape of the men's headgear.

'Friggin' Johnnie Rebs!' Seward snarled, and snapped off three more fast shots to empty his Colt.

'Hit the water!' Hedges yelled, kicked free of his stirrups and dived out of the saddle. He kept hold of the Spencer and the reins. His clothing and the weight of the spare ammunition in his pockets tried to drag him under. But, as an ordered fusillade of shots sent bullets snagging and hissing into the water around him, he lashed out with his feet. The horse hauled him along and his pumping legs helped to fight the drag.

Downriver, the others sought the insubstantial cover of the water and the more solid protection of their mounts. Much further away, Rhett become aware of how muted the gunfire now was and chanced a look back. Relief came close to exhileration as he saw he was no longer being pursued. All the activity save his own terror-inspired retreat was now centred at least a half-mile away. The bright moonlight clearly showed the group on the bank sending a hail of deadly fire towards the men and horses struggling across the river.

Then the New Englander commanded his own horse into a sharp turn, heading him for the river. His relief had been short-lived as a new fear gripped him. He was safe, but for how long? He was alone in Rebel territory and if he escaped the present danger, a fresh one could threaten at any moment.

His horse splashed into the water and he took a tighter grip with hands, feet and knees as the stallion launched into a frantic swim.

He didn't know how many of the Union men would reach the safety of the opposite bank. In different circumstances he would be glad to see them all die, for without exception he had a deep hatred of them. But war, especially with the enemy close at hand, made them his allies.

So, when his mount waded ashore on the north bank of the river, he wrenched on the reins and slammed in his heels to send the animal racing back along the shore line.

'For Christ's sake, some of you bastards stay alive,' he muttered, drawing his Colt and firing wildly while he was still far out of range.

Scott's horse took a bullet in the hindquarters and reared up out of the water. Then a second slug smashed through a bulging eye to find the brain. A forehoof came down hard on the head of Bell's mount, stunning the animal. Both troopers were forced to release their holds on the rope reins as the horses rolled. The men lashed frantically at the water with their arms and legs, letting go of the Spencers as they struggled against drowning.

First Forrest, then Seward fought their horses on to a different course. With bullets cracking over their heads and hissing into the water, they yelled to the swimming men, who kicked around and fastened grips on the offered saddles.

Hedges' mount was creased across the side of the neck. The wound had the effect of driving the animal into a faster swim. Then his pumping hooves plunged into the silt of the shallows and the Captain found himself being dragged along the river bed as the horse lashed and splashed up the bank. His one-handed grip on the reins stayed firm and abruptly he was out of the water, being hauled across a narrow, shingle beach. When brush began to snag at his clothes, he opened the hand.

The other two surviving horses dragged their burdens from the river and into the brush.

All five men who took a moment to regain their breath were aware of a slight change in the desperate situation. The firing from the opposite bank was as constant as ever, but fewer bullets cracked towards them. Then, simultaneously, Hedges and Forrest saw the reason. Pressed low in the brush, they looked across the river and saw that only half the fire power of the Rebels was directed at them. The rest of the soldiers were blasting lead on a different line.

'How about that?' Forrest muttered as he and the Captain swung their eyes to their own side of the river and saw Rhett galloping towards them, snapping off wild shots with his Spencer. 'The yellow bastard's doing it right for a change.'

A Rebel went down with a bullet in the head from Rhett's rifle. Then Hedges and Seward opened up, from cover towards a totally exposed enemy. Three more grey-uniformed forms slumped into inertness before the others ceased fire and lunged towards their mounts. Another died, toppling from his saddle, as the Rebels wheeled their horses and heeled them into a gallop back towards the cover of the stud farm.

Rhett hauled on his reins to bring the stallion to a shingle-showering halt on the beach in front of the brush.

'Hi, you guys!' he greeted with delighted relief as he surveyed the men on the ground, counting the full complement of five. 'Bet you figured I'd run out on you, uh?'

'Nah, Bob,' Seward said with a grin as he slotted fresh shells into the Spencer. 'We knew you'd back us up.'

'Only natural you'd be a little behind,' Scott added with a giggle.

'Real smart trick, Bob,' Forrest complimented, bringing a grin back to the New Englander's face, to replace the grimace he showed in response to the barbed humour.

Hedges, his rifle fully-loaded again, ignored the men and peered back up and across the river towards the stud farm. They had killed only a handful of the Rebels and the rest were all back at the farm: some still mounted in a group on the trail running past the front of the house, others inside.

'You got any more up your sleeve, trooper?' he asked when his survey was completed and he raked his gaze to look at the mounted New Englander.

'What's that, Captain?' Rhett asked, bewildered.

'Any more smart tricks. Only need the one – to get Douglas away from the Rebs, if he's still alive.'

'He took his chances like the rest of us,' Seward growled. 'I say we high-tail it outta here now we got the chance. How about you, Frank?'

'You got an idea, Billy,' the mean-faced sergeant said softly.

'So let's get,' Seward urged, standing up.

Forrest rose only as far as a squat on his haunches. 'In talkin' about high-tail,' he growled, and showed his brown teeth in a wry grin. He looked at Hedges. 'Rhett don't keep his tricks up his sleeves, Captain.'

All of the men except Hedges and Forrest had been as anxious as Seward to take it on the run again. But now their mood soured as they realised the Sergeant was not yet prepared to assume command.

'Speak your piece,' Hedges invited.

'Your move, sir,' Forrest answered with a shrug. 'It just figures that all Rhett's tricky deals are gonna be off the bottom.'

'STAY mounted, lady,' the new sheriff of Monksville said. 'And you guys get up slow and unbuckle your gunbelts.'

'If we don't?' Melody Devine challenged.

'I start blasting.'

'At an unarmed woman?'

'Guess.'

She still had her back to him as she sat her horse in the centre of the square, peering over her shoulder through the falling dusk. It took her just a second to reach the decision. Then she swung her head around to glare at her brothers.

'Do like he says!' she ordered. 'He's not kidding.'

Lon and Clayton glanced at each other, but found their gaze drawn back to the angry face of their sister. The Bowie knife was dropped, then the two men straightened up, took off their gunbelts and allowed them to fall to the ground. Not until then did Gerstenberg push wide the batswings to hurry out into the square, leading the doddering town councillors and every other aged customer from the saloon. Other doors opened around the square to give exit to the horrified and curious watchers. And lamps were lit to spill yellow illumination out on to the square, holding back the encroachment of night.

Edge, the rifle lowered to his hip, kept ahead of the crowd. He halted beside the woman.

'Off, and into the law office, lady,' he ordered.

She showed him a look of angry confidence that stopped short of bravado. Then she swung down to the ground, always covered by the rifle, which acted to hold her brothers inactive.

'You won't get a conviction, mister hard man,' she taunted.

'Ain't my job,' he replied, nudging her in the small of the back with the Winchester muzzle.

As she headed for the still-darkened law office, he nodded for Lon and Clayton to lead the way. They did, and as soon they cleared the area around the terribly injured Andrews, the townspeople crowded around the rear of the stage.

The law office had only a single cell, at the rear through an archway. The door was still open from when the last prisoner was dragged out.

'He's the only thing we have to fear,' Melody warned sharply as she saw her brothers glance at the rack of rifles behind the desk.

The men did not reply and led the way into the cell. Their sister entered behind them and Edge used the barrel of the rifle to swing the door closed. The key – one of a bunch on a metal ring – was still in the lock. He turned it and withdrew it.

'There's only one cot in here!' Melody complained as the half-breed went back through the archway.

He struck a match, lit the lamp on the desk and then opened the pot-bellied stove in a corner of the office. 'Only got the job for a day,' he answered as he started to set a fire in the cleaned-out stove. 'Won't have the time to do any refurnishing.'

'We'll manage, sis,' Clayton growled sourly. 'Just for the one night.'

'That's right!' Melody agreed, the complaining tone gone from her voice. 'Judge Hewitt's always liked me. When he hears what Andrews did to me, he's sure to tell the jury what verdict to bring in.'

The fire blazing fiercely from the kindling and started to get a grip on the fuel and Edge closed up the stove door, stepping back. He sat on the side of the desk, from where he could be seen by the three prisoners.

'What do you think about that, mister new sheriff?' Lon taunted. 'No matter what a jury of those old has-beens out there try to do, the judge'll set us free. 'Cause he's got a hankerin' for Melody, here.'

'No accounting for taste,' the half-breed replied wryly,

and glanced through the archway. All three Devines were sitting on the cot.

Anger flared across the faces of the men, but the woman accepted the taunt with resignation.

'You'll see,' she retorted evenly.

But she had lost the half-breed, who had returned into the state of pre-occupation that had gripped him for so long, whenever outside circumstances did not affect him. He moved around to the back of the desk and dropped into the leather-covered swivel chair. The rifle he rested across the uncluttered desk top. The office door was still open, but with the heat of the stove beginning to make itself felt, he did not close it. Through the doorway, he had a wide angle view of the square as Andrews was carried gently across it. But he saw and digested the scene with only a part of his mind, for the major share of his thought process was concerned with the telegraph in his billfold.

It was now obvious that the message had been nothing more than bait to bring him to Monksville. Nancy Harman, who could have told him why he had been tricked into coming to the town, was dead. And she had evidently not revealed this to her brother until today – when he returned from the Funeral Mountains Way Station and mentioned that a man named Edge was out there waiting for the stage. For if the sheriff had known the story that morning, he would surely have attempted an arrest with the backing of a whole posse.

So, if Nancy had kept the secret from her brother, it was unlikely she had told anyone else in town.

'Sheriff, we gonna get fed in this dump?' Lon Devine demanded.

Edge ignored the question. All he knew was that a lawman was on his way from Kansas, to arrest him for an old murder. A killing committed just after the close of the War Between The States, and the only one for which a warrant had been issued against him. A warrant in the name of Captain Josiah C. Hedges. Thus, he had two pieces of information to work on – the man who was coming for him knew that Edge was really Hedges, and he also knew of the marriage to Beth. More than that, even: knew of the depth of feeling Edge had for his dead wife – deep and strong enough to hook him on the bait of an unexplained telegraph that mentioned her.

'Hey, I said are we gonna get fed?' Lon yelled.

'Sure you'll get fed, if you can face eatin' after what you did.'

It was Gerstenberg who snarled the response, as he entered the law office. He was short of breath from carrying Edge's gear, which he dumped on the floor just inside the doorway. He crossed to the desk and dropped the badge beside the Winchester.

'For the money we're payin', you can at least wear that,' he said in the same tone he had used on Lon Devine.

'Two questions, feller,' the half-breed said, not touching the badge.

'If one of them's about your money, town treasurer's over in the courthouse now, openin' up the civic safe. A thousand in advance and the balance when your tour of duty is over.'

'No sweat,' the half-breed allowed, his lean face still set in a pensive expression. Then he grinned. 'You're pretty good in the prediction line. Takes care of one of my questions.'

The night air coming in through the open doorway now had a very cold bite to it. The elderly mayor went to the stove, splaying out his hands towards it. 'Man don't get to my age without gettin' an understandin' of his fellow men, Mr Edge. I'll make another guess – that you don't plan to ask about the Andrews boy. But I'll tell you anyway. Doc reckons he's got a fifty-fifty chance. He's a strong boy.'

'Who won't grow up to be a man!' Melody called harshly from the cell.

Edge ignored Gerstenberg's report, the woman's comment and the raucous laughter it drew from her brothers. 'You know anything about a telegraph Nancy Harman sent me?' he asked.

The mayor showed the same brand of disinterest in the half-breed's question as Edge had displayed in the news about Andrews' condition. He shook his head absently. 'Can't send telegraphs from Monksville. No line into town. Most of the folks that live here ain't got no time for new-fangled things like that. Nearest telegraph office is at Angus Wells, day's ride south.'

'What d'you know about the Harman woman?'

'Came from Kansas, like her brother did. But a lot later and only for a visit. Been here less than three weeks.'

Edge nodded. It fitted, if the lawman coming after him was more intent on killing him than arresting him. Far outside his own jurisdiction he could gun a man down without news of the act getting back to his home ground and jeopardising whatever position he had there.

'Obliged,' the half-breed said.

'All aboard!' the voice of Mort yelled out in the square. 'Stage is headin' out. Angus Wells next stop.'

Then a whip cracked, hooves thudded at the hard ground and wheels began to turn. Dust was raised and some of it drifted through the open doorway into the law office.

'My belly's beginnin' to think my throat's been cut,' Lon Devine whined.

'It's a nice idea,' the half-breed drawled, as he picked up the tin star and pinned it to his chest.

Gerstenberg scowled. He pointed at the badge. 'That means your job is to protect every citizen in this town, sheriff,' he reminded. 'Those three prisoners included.'

Edge grinned. 'A man can only do his best, feller.'

'For two grand a day, you better be the best,' the mayor muttered, relinquishing his warm position at the stove and heading for the door. He stopped, shot a contemptuous glance at the half-breed, then stepped out into the night, which had become quiet again now that Mort had driven the clattering stage far beyond earshot.

'You screwed these decrepit old bastards outta two thousand dollars for a day's work?' Clayton Devine yelled incredulously.

Edge leaned back in his chair and raised his booted feet up on to the desk. 'And I'm obliged to you for your help. Couldn't have done it without you.'

'Keep your thanks and everything else!' Melody snarled.

'Yeah!' Clayton agreed.

'Intend to,' Edge told them as he took out the makings. 'Anyway, you've already had your cut.'

CHAPTER FIVE

CORPORAL Hal Douglas was afraid. As he ran across the meadow and saw the Union troopers gallop away from him, he had started to scream curses at them. Then, as the bunch of Rebel soldiers angled towards him, his voice dropped and he muttereed inarticulate pleas for God to forgive him for battering the aged monk to death. He was aware of the Spencer in his hands and the captured Colt in his belt. But he knew he was not going to reach the horse Hedges had turned loose in the corral: and he thought his life might be spared if he did not fire at the Rebels.

He purposely hurled the rifle away as he tripped to the turf, and yelled that he intended to surrender. But the thud of hooves and slap of leather drowned his croaking, breathless voice. And the soldiers who rode their horses up to him thought he was fumbling for his Colt to get off a shot. A veteran sergeant leapt from his mount and launched a vicious kick that split the skin under the greasy hair above Douglas' right ear. The Union man was plunged into unconsciousness and so, for awhile, was unable to experience anything.

He returned to awareness in the hallway of the farmhouse, and smelt the familiar bitter-sweet odour of new death and faded gunsmoke. He felt pain first, then opened his eyes and the fear swept back – far more terrifying than that which he had experienced out in the meadow. He was bound at the ankles and knees and his hands and arms were lashed to his chest. They had dumped him on his side, the temple and cheek stiff with crusted blood uppermost. He had recognised the men as Confederate soldiers as they galloped towards him, so it was no shock to see the uniforms now. A captain and two sergeants, supervising six enlisted men who had draped the dead in blankets and were carrying them out through the front door of the house.

There was no more gunfire and Douglas was certain his despair was complete – that the Rebs had killed or captured the whole unit. Not that it mattered. If every one of the bastards had got away, they would run out on him. None of them had even given a damn for him.

'Sir, he's awake,' the sergeant reported.

All the Rebels turned hate-filled eyes towards Douglas, who swallowed down a threat of nausea and fixed one thought in his mind. Whatever they did to him, he must not admit to being a Union soldier. Because he was in civilian clothing deep inside enemy territory they would think him a spy, which meant he was subject to summary execution.

'You!' the middle-aged captain snapped, pointing a gloved finger at Douglas. 'Will be taken to town and handed over to the civil authorities. You'll be charged with the murder of the old man in the woods and an accessory to the killings which took place here.'

Douglas groaned. So they had found the dead monk. News of it was sure to get back to the monastery and his true identity would then be known.

'Take him out and put him on a horse,' the officer ordered.

The enlisted men were busy with the dead, so it was the two non-coms who hoisted Douglas roughly from the floor. And, as he swung painfully between them, the Union man began to sob. For he knew he was destined to die – by civil or military law. It didn't matter. He was in an inescapable trap with the shadow of the gallows on every side of him.

Withdrawn into his misery and terror, Hal Douglas saw nothing of his surroundings as he was carried out into the bright moonlit night and folded, face-down, across the saddle of a horse. He was tied on to the animal, alongside the dead monk brought out of the timber. He was unaware of this body, or the corpses of the six shot soldiers who had been killed on the river bank. Nor of the blanket-wrapped remains of the three men and one woman who had been blasted to death in the farmhouse. He did not see the string of six colts and five stallions that were lined out behind the columns of twos into which the soldiers formed. Only on the very periphery of his awareness did he sense the motion of the horse beneath him as the column moved off – back along the trail which curved towards the low-sided gorge.

Hedges saw all of this as he lay sprawled out flat on the high ground above the trail on the south side of the river. He was breathless from leading his men on a fast run through the cover on the north bank, and his clothing was sopping from a second swim across the river. Behind and below him, the men were similarly breathless and soaked to the skin as they crouched among the boulders at the side of the trail. He could hear their sour-toned voices.

'I don't like leaving my horse over the other side,' Rhett complained. 'I'm the only man kept his mount and I gotta leave him. He'll likely bolt if there's a ruckus, high-breed animal like that.'

'Bob?' Forrest said.

'Yeah, Frank?'

'One, you ain't a man. Two, there's a whole friggin' bunch of trained cavalry mounts comin' down the trail. Three, just make sure you don't bolt when the ruckus starts. Four, you don't stop whinin', I'm gonna forget you're on my side.'

'For once I'm with Bob,' Billy Seward growled. 'Six of us got across with four horses. And those Rebs weren't comin' after us. We had it made.'

'Yeah,' Bell agreed. 'Until the friggin' Captain took it into his head to blow the whole deal on account of Hal.'

When the head of the Rebel column had closed to within two hundred yards of the mouth of the gorge, Hedges pushed himself back from his vantage point, staying pressed hard against the tough grass.

'The Captain ain't no hero!' Forrest snarled softly as he heard the clop of many hooves. 'You guys have been through enough with him to know that. He don't do nothin' 'less there's a friggin' solid reason for it. Like now, you lunkheads. You reckon he gives a shit for Hal's hide? He gives about as much of a damn as you do. But them Rebs didn't come after us 'cause they think we're just ordinary horsethieves. Which makes us the problem of the local law.'

'So?' John Scott wanted to know as Hedges moved down into the scattering of boulders.

Everyone looked at the Captain, but Forrest wasn't inhibited by his presence.

'So, you stupid sonsofbitches!' he snarled. 'For the first time in his useless life, Douglas is important. Tell 'em, sir.'

The accuracy of Forrest's reasoning was the latest example of his instinctive ability to lead.

'The corporal has one slender chance of saving his skin,' Hedges said as he crouched down and levered a shell into the Spencer. 'When the chips are down, he'll start to shoot off his mouth.'

'Right!' Forrest cut in. 'He'll tell the Rebs who he is and who we are. I reckon they'll string him up anyway, do some figurin' about us and send every spare man out huntin' for us.'

The four enlisted men shrugged and grimaced, unconvinced that this was the true motive. But a glower from Forrest and an impassive look from Hedges sent them to their designated positions as the sound of approaching riders swelled.

'And remember,' the Captain rasped. 'Just one Johnnie Reb escapes, it'll make you right and me wrong.'

'It might just be worth it,' Seward growled, but low enough so that only Scott and Bell on either side of him heard the comment.

Then the Union men became silent and still in their hiding places, spread out at three yard intervals along the trail. For the Rebel troop, come to buy horses from the stud farm, were heading into the gorge. They didn't have as many as they had been ordered to collect, and had paid with the lives of six of their number instead of Confederate dollars. The troop had comprised nineteen men. Now, as they held their own mounts, the pack animals and the depleted new stock to a steady walk on the trail between the strewn boulders and the river, there were just thirteen of them left.

It was an unlucky number.

Hedges fired the opening shot from ambush, but the others had taken first pressure on the triggers of their weapons and five more reports sounded as one an instant after the deadly signal.

The Rebel captain died without knowledge of what was happening. He was staring straight ahead, his mind concerned with the report he would have to give to his commanding officer. A single murdering horsethief for the loss of six fully-trained troopers was in no way a good bargain. Then the bullet burst through his cheek, angled up into his brain and shattered the top of his skull to make its exit. Rhett shot one of the sergeants in the side and got lucky. The bullet glanced off a rib and found the non-com's heart. The New Englander spent part of a second wishing it was Forrest who went sideways out of the saddle. Scott and Bell, their rifles at the bottom of the river, had to use the smaller calibre Colts. Two Rebel troopers went backwards off their mounts with blood blossoming over their uniforms from the holes in their stomachs. Forrest and Seward chose head shots. The sergeant's bullet smashed into a victim's nose, bored a hole through it and burrowed into the ear of the soldier riding alongside him. Seward scored a hit at his target's throat and saw the man's Adam's apple plop out of the blood-torrenting wound.

All these Rebels save the officer had a split-second's notice of what was about to happen. For, as the captain was blasted from his horse by his Union opposite number, every mounted man raked fear-filled eyes towards the boulders. And they saw the six water-logged men rise up and aim guns from a range of no more than four feet.

Abruptly, the gorge was filled with the confusing sounds of panic. Wounded men screamed in competition with the cries of their frightened comrades. Horses snorted and reared. Men cursed their animals and their attackers. Four men were sprawled dead on the ground amid the lashing, pumping hooves. Three more writhed in the agony of their wounds.

Then, as the surviving Rebel sergeant yelled an order, he and his men released reins and lead lines so that they could leap out of their saddles as they drew their guns. The Union men's guns cracked a second time and only Bell and Scott scored fatal hits. Two Rebels ceased to lunge and became limp, flopping hard to the ground. The bullets lodged in their hearts ensured they did not feel the pain as their faces smashed against the rocks.

The Sergeant knocked aside Hedges' Spencer as he leapt at the Captain. But his own revolver snagged on the holster and Hedges beat him to the draw as the weight of the man staggered him backwards. The Spencer exploded a wild shot to the side, driving lead into the head of a bolting horse. Then, as the Sergeant finally got his revolver free, one hand clawing for Hedges' slitted eyes, the Captain pressed the muzzle of the Colt into the non-com's belly and squeezed the trigger.

The Rebel staggered backwards, clutching at himself. 'Jesus, that hurt!' he groaned, remembered he had his gun out now, and tried to level it.

'Go tell him personally,' Hedges rasped, and shot the sergeant in the heart.

Rhett was a moment from death. He was flat on his back with a Rebel kneeling on his stomach. His assailent had a revolver pressed against the New Englander's throat. Rhett's mouth was gaping and his strident scream cut across every other sound in the gorge.

Hedges, Scott and Bell whirled towards the sound at the same moment, levelled Colts dragging only fractionally behind their searching stares. The three revolvers cracked in unison and the Rebel's head seemed to explode under the impact of the bullets. A great deal of the showering blood and several pieces of torn flesh and splintered bone hit Rhett in the face. He gagged on the taste of warm gore that entered his screaming mouth.

Scott grinned at Bell. 'Thought his kind liked eating head,' he rasped.

Then both whirled around to search for new victims.

'Take care of the wounded!' Hedges yelled at them and they leapt across the boulders on to the trail, knowing exactly what the order meant.

Forrest and a Rebel were locked in mutual bearhugs, struggling for possession of a single Colt. Hedges reached the locked-together men in four long strides, hand streaking away from the back of his neck. The moon glinted on the blade of the razor, but the shine did not match the brightness of the killer look in the narrowed eyes.

'The bastard's mine!' Forrest yelled.

But Hedges punched a hand between the two men and withdrew it just as fast. The honed edge of the razor slashed a lethally deep cut in the Rebel's throat and he started to fall.

'Make war, not love,' the Captain rasped.

As the man slackened his grip, the life bubbling out of him, Forrest roared an obscenity and sent a bullet into the moistly gurgling mouth. Then he glared malevolently at Hedges, whirled, and saw Seward.

The young, baby-faced killer had his man backed up against a large boulder. The Rebel was twice his age and bigger and heavier. Blood was running from a gash on Seward's temple and the Rebel trooper was trembling as he prepared to take the punishment for opening up the wound.

'You're a bastard, you know that?' Seward rasped, aiming his Spencer at the man's saliva-run mouth. 'All Rebs are friggin' bastards. But the friggin' bastards who make me bleed are the worst kind of friggin' bastards.'

'Just kill him, trooper!' Hedges barked.

'Aw, let him be, Captain,' Forrest defended, his anger subsiding as a mean grin spread across his face. 'He's fightin' for the Union. Gives him the right to make a Federal case outta it.'

'I bleed, you bleed worse, you friggin' bastard,' Seward intoned, apparently deaf to the voices of his superiors.

Then he altered the aim of his rifle and fired two fast shots. First the terrified man's right knee was shattered, then the left. The man screamed and fell to the ground.

Two more shots emptied the Spencer and smashed the Rebel's elbows.

Forrest, with the grin still in place, and Hedges, whose killer look was transforming into an expression of disgust, raked their eyes away from Seward as he dropped the Spencer and drew his Colt. Scott and Bell had found four wounded men, too weak to resist. They had dragged them, face-down, to the mud at the river's edge and were standing on the necks of the helpless men. All four died, smothered by the thick ooze that was sucked into their windpipes. Abruptly, Rhett leapt from the rocks, raced across the corpse-littered trail and went headlong into the water to wash the blood from his face and mouth.

'He's one of ours, for our sins,' Forrest growled at Scott and Bell as Seward fired another shot.

Blood spurted from a fresh wound in the man the youngster had at his mercy, and yet he still lived. But Hedges knew better than to interfere. For it was in situations like this that his command over the men was at its most tenuous. He killed the enemy with the same brand of excited lust as the others but the exhilaration drained out of him immediately the job was finished. The men, once they had the upper hand, nurtured the way they felt and were determined to draw the last grain of pleasure from it. To try to curtail their enjoyment was to risk a mutiny: and if these men mutinied, killing Hedges would be the first act in the spontaneous plan.

So the Captain swung away from the brutal scene, striding deeper into the gorge, where a bunch of horses had halted and were standing nervously. And he once again rationalised the men's behaviour. They were soldiers in a bitter war and killing was their prime function. That they got so much satisfaction from slaughter was why they made such excellent soldiers. And the manner of the enemy's dying was immaterial in the overall context of war. Just as long as they died.

A last shot crashed into the centre of the Rebel's forehead and his groans of agony were silenced.

'Did I make him pay, or did I make him pay?' Seward yelled.

'Disarmed and without a leg to stand on, Billy!' Forrest answered happily. 'He had to get the death sentence.'

'And Rog and me sure rubbed these guys' faces in it!' Scott boasted.

Rhett, all traces of blood washed from his face, sat up in the river and splashed excitedly at the water, like a young child in his bath. 'I killed me a sergeant, I killed me a sergeant!' he chanted joyfully.

Forrest spat. 'Ain't he somethin' else?' he growled to anybody who cared to answer.

'Don't we all know it?' Seward replied with a giggle.

The excitement of the killing and the heat of his anger gone, Hedges was calm again. Forrest had been only half right in guessing his reasoning for setting the ambush. The easy killings at the farm had gone part way to bolstering the men's morale after the long lay-off. But now, after the massacre in the gorge, their spirits had soared to the zenith again. They had proved they were the best fighting unit in the war and were at the peak of readiness to go on proving it. All he had to do was make sure they had the opportunities and his command status was intact.

'Gee, Captain, I just knew you'd come back for me,' Douglas croaked and his voice put the complete seal of success on the operation.

As the men approached the bunch of nervous horses, Hedges went in among the animals and located the one with two forms slumped across it. He didn't have to lift up the head of the dead man. The cowled habit marked the body as that of the dead monk. The congealed blood on the head covering told of the manner of his dying. Hedges crouched down at the side of the horse and stared up into the blood-crusted face of the Union man.

'I told you to turn him loose, corporal,' he said softly. 'Why'd you kill him?'

Douglas' happiness drained from his features and he found he was as afraid of Hedges as of the Rebels who had captured him. He thought fleetingly of lying, but had the unreasonable dread that the slitted blue eyes could see clear through into his brain. He gulped. 'He got me mad, sir. He reckoned there was good in all men. I don't like arguin' with a guy who don't know what he's talkin' about.'

Hedges nodded and stood up, taking out his razor. Slowly this time. He saw the others approaching: and the slumped, shattered and bloodied bodies strewn across the trail and over the rocks. He started to cut Douglas loose.

'Hey!' Rhett said, pointing to the body folded over the horse. 'The monk's dead.'

'He won't be tellin' heaven nothin' good about us, that's for sure,' Bell growled.

'You waste him, Hal?' Seward wanted to know, as the freed Douglas slid to the ground and stood there unsteadily, massaging the use back into his cramped limbs.

'The monk was crazy,' Hedges answered sadly. 'Douglas beat some sense into him.'

Forrest moved up to the horse and lifted the cowl, exposing the massive wound in the father abbot's skull. 'Hal give him a pretty strong argument,' he muttered with his tobacco-stained teeth displayed in an evil grin.

'He was pretty crazy,' Hedges answered, matching the sergeant's expression of black humour. 'But at least he died for his belief.'

Only Douglas was in a position to share the wryness of the comment, but he was too concerned with his own discomfort and was oblivious to all else.

'In God?' Forrest asked as he allowed the cowl to fall back into place.

'In men.'

The sergeant didn't understand, but he laughed. 'A habit he got into, maybe?'

'Somethin' to do with his ordered way of life?' Rhett suggested with a guffaw.

'Yeah!' Bell growled. 'That's why he bought it from the back. The monk went into retreat.'

THE treasurer brought Edge the promised thousand dollars and left without saying a word. The half-breed counted the money to pass the time. The three prisoners took it in turns to demand food and were ignored by the patient sheriff. But Gerstenberg had apparently paid heed to the earlier complaint, for as the courthouse clock struck the hour of seven, the lanky bartender from the saloon kicked at the now closed door of the law office.

Edge ambled across to open it and saw the man carried a tray with a cloth draped over it. The bartender was as nervous as the treasurer had been.

'Steak, beans and grits for three,' he said.

'Somebody can't count,' Edge answered.

The bartender swallowed hard and thrust the tray towards him. 'I don't give the orders, sheriff. Just take 'em. Mayor reckoned that at your pay you don't get all found. Said just the three suppers for the prisoners.'

The half-breed took the tray. 'I'm ordering one more. Bring it.'

The tall, thin man gulped again, nodded and turned away. Edge kicked the door closed to block out the cold night and carried the tray through the arch at the rear of the office.

'About damn time!' Lon growled. 'Folks could starve for all you care.'

Melody showed Edge a taunting smile. 'They also serve who only stand and wait,' she said.

The half-breed set the tray down on the floor and drew off the cloth. The steaks looked good and there was plenty on the side. 'I ain't waiting, lady,' he told her and picked up one of the plates and a knife and fork. Then he straightened and slid the tray under the high-hung door with his foot.

'You're real tough with these bars between us!' Clayton snarled. 'Or with a rifle in your hands.'

'I'm a real tiger,' the half-breed agreed. 'The hungry kind right now.'

He carried the plate to the desk and sat down to eat. It was as good as it looked. The prisoners muttered among themselves. Edge didn't know who was left out, but he or she wasn't denied for long. The bartender returned with another plate in less than five minutes.

'Take it through,' Edge told him, waving his fork.

'That ain't my job,' the bartender protested nervously, peering across the office and through the archway. 'Gettin' close to prisoners.'

Edge chewed some steak. 'Put up your right hand.'

'Uh?'

'Just do it.'

The bartender transferred the plate to his left hand and complied.

'I formally swear you in as a deputy for one minute,' Edge drawled. Then he grinned. 'If any of those three back there try anything, yell. It'll be an attack on a duly elected peace officer. No sweat. I'll just kill them.'

'Real friggin' tough!' Lon muttered.

The nervous bartender adopted Edge's method of pushing the plate through the gap under the door. But he stood much further back. Then he left the office fast.

For a while, only the scrape of metal on china disturbed the peace of the law office. Outside, the town was as quiet as the whole of Death Valley and the twin ranges of mountains that formed it. The advanced years of the great majority of its popuation decreed that Monksville bedded down early.

'You're a waiter, sheriff,' Melody said suddenly. 'It's why you're here – a man like you in a place like this. Waiting for somebody.'

Edge had his feet back up on the desk, hat tipped forward over his forehead. 'What's your interest.'

'Just making conversation,' the woman answered indifferently. 'These two aren't any company at all.'

The half-breed became aware of the gentle snoring issuing from the cell. 'We got nothing to talk about, lady. You've attended to your business and I'll take care of mine when it comes.'

'He really did rape me,' she said insistently.

'Ain't arguing the fact.'

'Knocked me out, tied me up and gagged me, then did it.'

Edge said nothing.

'He had no cause to do that. I led him on a bit, maybe, but it was only in fun. He just suddenly went crazy, you know?'

The half-breed recalled how Andrews had lost control of his temper out at the way station. 'Tell the judge,' he said dully.

'I intend to,' Melody replied with heavy emphasis. 'But I reckon you're a man who fights his own battles without running to the law all the time. You ought to be able to understand why I made my brothers do what they did.'

'Never had a sister,' he told her. 'If I did . . . '

'What?' Melody asked anxiously.

'I'd maybe be like your brothers.'

'Willing to take revenge on the man who dishonoured her, sheriff?'

'Be able to sleep through her yapping.'

'You bastard!' she snarled.

Edge grinned to himself at the sudden change of tone.

'Sheriff!' a man yelled out in the square, his tone high with fear. 'Sheriff, the Andrews kid has gone!'

Edge swept his feet off the desk and slammed them to the floor to power himself erect, snatching the Winchester from where it rested.

'Hey, you stay here and protect us!' Melody shrieked. 'Lon, Clayton!'

He shot a glance through the archway as he took long strides towards the door. The two brothers were slumped crosswise on the cot, backs against the wall and chins resting on their chests. The woman sat between them and they came awake cursing as she clawed their shoulders and shook them. He jerked open the door and flinched at the chill air stream that hit him in the face. Moonlight was bright beyond the deep patches of shadow thrown by buildings and trees. A man, small, rotund and white-faced was angling towards the law office from the start of the street on the south side. He wore a long nightshirt and carpet slippers. Lights sprang from windows and drapes were drawn aside to allow faces to peer out. The courthouse clock began to chime the hour of nine.

'Thank God!' the small man gasped breathlessly when he saw Edge silhouetted in the law office doorway. 'I'm Doc Hartmann.' He halted short of the sidewalk and took in great gulps of air. 'Taking care of the injured man at my house. He's real sick and I sedated him. Thought he'd sleep solid the night through.'

Doors opened and people emerged on to the streets and the square. Mostly men who had donned robes over their nightwear.

'What's that you say?' Gerstenberg demanded, his voice booming out above the excited mutterings of the curious.

Hartmann half-turned and began to shiver with the cold. 'Andrews has gone, Scott!' he gasped. 'God knows how he had the strength.'

The mayor halted alongside the doctor and glowered at Edge. 'Don't just stand there, man, go find him!' he snarled.

'Figure he'll find me,' the half-breed replied evenly.

'For two grand a day, you do what I tell you!' Gerstenberg bellowed.

Edge sighed, canted the Winchester across his shoulder and used his free hand to ease the pin of the star out of his shirt. Gerstenberg and Hartmann, with the crowd gathered behind them, stared in horrified awe as the half-breed flipped the badge across the sidewalk and into the dust of the square.

'What you doin'?' the mayor demanded, his voice suddenly croaky.

Edge drew out his billfold. 'Deal was, I handled the job my way, feller. Did that for about four hours. At the daily rate you're paying, I figure I've earned three-thirty give or take a few bucks. You got some money coming back to – '

'Okay!' Gerstenberg yelled. 'Your way.'

'Sheriff!' Melody Devine screamed.

'No, don't!' one of her brothers pleaded.

Edge scowled at the mayor and whirled. Two shots rang out as he turned and a third blasted lead into the cell as he slammed the Winchester stock to his shoulder and pumped the action. The haggard, deathly-pale face of Andrews framed in the barred cell window was abruptly splashed with vivid red as the rifle exploded. The gush of blood came from the hole above his right eye. Then the youngster was thrown backwards by the impact of the killing bullet. His dead hand released the Deane-Harding 54 bore double-action revolver and it hit the cement floor of the cell as his body thudded to the ground outside.

Edge crossed the law office in long strides and peered coldly into the cell.

'I was goin' to tell you he took my gun!' Hartmann wailed.

The three prisoners had been lined up at the cell bars, anxious to hear what was being said out in the square. But Andrews had blasted them to the floor. Three head shots that had spilled a lot of blood which even now widened its massive pool around the slumped bodies. Lon and Clayton had taken the bullets squarely in the skull and the only movement from their crumpled forms was the oozing trickle of escaping blood from the hair-covered wounds. Melody was slumped between her brothers, an ugly gouge across her neck, and the lower half of her right ear hanging from the upper section by a mere tendon. The bullet had smashed into a cell bar and bounced back. It lay, a misshapen wad of lead, beside the revolver under the window. The woman breathed raggedly in unconsciousness.

Footfalls thudded on the law office floor.

'Are they dead?' the mayor gasped.

'Her brothers have joined the heavenly chorus,' the half-breed muttered. 'But Melody lingers on.'

CHAPTER SIX

THE seven Union troopers re-crossed the river on captured Rebel horses and re-armed with confiscated weapons and spare ammunition. Flushed with success and with the adrenalin pumping forcefully through their bodies, all but one were looking for new trouble. Only Hedges controlled a tendency towards over-confidence and, because of the way in which he had handled the ambush and its aftermath, he was able to exert a firm influence over the men. He was in complete command again and knew they would follow wherever he chose to lead them. All he had to do was keep them on the move and anticipate the threat of trouble which the terrain ahead of them them might hold.

For the massacre at the gorge would not remain undiscovered for long and the strength of the forces sent in pursuit of the ambushers would be as large as if Douglas had named them as Union troopers. So, strategically, the slaughter had been no more than a delaying tactiç. Thus did Hedges drive the men hard, every horse stride taking them away from the pursuit that would inevitably begin.

Trouble – even a minor skirmish – would be to the advantage of the pursuers. Thus did Hedges maintain a constant watch into the far, moonlit distance and swing wide whenever a sign of habitation showed: be it an isolated farmstead or a Virginian town. Always he made the detour to the west, knowing that the broad lower reaches of the Potomac River barred the south-eastern approach to Washington but ignorant of whether or not the Federal Army was in possession of both banks.

As the night wore on, weariness and hunger began to dampen the men's spirits. It was nothing they said, for the rapid pace set by Hedges allowed little time for talk. But the Captain sensed the mood change, aided by the fact that the long trek and lack of food since leaving the monastery had started to have an adverse effect on his concentration. And concentration was important, for he had no personal knowledge of the country they were travelling and no maps. He broke the trail by following the stars and relying on dim recollections of plans and charts he had seen years before.

Then, as the first light of the false dawn streaked the eastern skyline, he could only make a half-educated guess that the large town far to the right was Fredericksburg. Make the guess and curse his ignorance of how the war had progressed during the many months he and the men had been behind enemy lines. For Fredericksburg could well be in Union hands, because they had seen no Rebel uniforms since the gorge: but neither had they seen a Federal soldier.

He dropped the pace to an easy canter up a long incline of broken ground and heard Rhett's complaining tones.

'Ought to start gettin' cold soon, you guys. We must be close to the friggin' North Pole by this time.'

'Sure hope that ain't so, Bob,' Scott answered wearily. 'For your sake.'

'Yeah,' Bell countered. 'I hear the weather's so bad up there it can freeze a man's ass off.'

'Then how will you make it after this war's over?' Douglas asked.

'Have to stick to being a handyman,' Seward said with a giggle.

'For cryin' out loud, lay off me for once,' Rhett groaned.

'Hey, the fruit's turned sour,' Scott growled.

Hedges reined his horse to a half at the top of the rise. 'That look like the North Pole?' he asked as the men stopped their horses at either side of him.

'Hey, he's right,' Seward said. 'Should have knowed the Captain wouldn't snow us.'

What the men saw spread before them was an old battlefield; what was left of a vast area of what had once been dense woodland snaked with a few roads connecting small farmsteads. Occasional patches of timber still stood strong and tall but, for the most part, the country had been ravaged by heavy artillery and forest fire. Dead trees leaned at crazy angles or lay on the ground, stripped of the last vestiges of foliage. Once thick underbrush had been reduced to grey ash and black soot. Half a dozen scattered farmsteads could be seen in the brightening dawn, surrounded by fields which were either burnt out or choked with weeds. Old bullet scars marked some of the walls and shell holes gaped in the roofs. As the morning dew began to evaporate, it released the familiar odours of expended gunpowder, burned wood, human excrement and decayed flesh. All the troopers had fought in their share of battles and had they smelled this scene before they saw it, they would have known what had taken place here.

'Looks like they been carrying on the war without us,' Forrest said, and spat as if he resented the fact.

The men had spent a long time surveying the arena in which the bloody and vicious Battle of The Wilderness had been fought, some six weeks earlier. Perhaps a full minute, and then the abrupt intrusion of Forrest's bitter-toned voice emphasised the utter silence clamped over the battlefield. Not even from the unscathed clumps of timber did a single bird attempt a plaintive note of the dawn chorus.

'We've eaten in worse places than that,' Hedges said, pointing to the closest farmstead, a mile distant and due north. Its barn was a heap of charred planks and there were bullet and shell holes in the roof and walls of the house, but the surrounding fields had escaped the torch.

Forrest looked up into the brightening sky, where not a hint of cloud showed. 'And it ain't gonna rain, Captain.'

Both men heeled their horses forward and the troopers were only a moment behind them. The ground fell away as gently as it had risen on the far side. Then they were in The Wilderness, even more desolate after the battle than it had been before. For half a mile the hooves of the horses kicked up a dust of ash and soot. Then the men rode along a narrow trail which curved around to sweep across the front of the farmstead property.

The fencing had been torn down and trampled in the ebb and flow of the battle, and the men leapt their horses across the line of splintered wood and galloped them across a field.

'And we've eaten worse things than turnips,' Seward called, recognising the crop struggling to survive amid the thriving weeds.

They slowed and reined their horses to a halt in the small yard before the single-storey frame-built house. The door was firmly closed, but entry would be easy for there was not a single panc of unbroken glass in any of the windows. While the men sat and looked at the house, Hedges eased his horse over to a well. The rope was played out down into the murky depths and he began to wind the handle.

'Ain't we people suffered enough?' a woman called.

A gunshot punctuated the reedy-voiced complaint and Hedges released the winding handle. The bullet bit dust out of the circle of bricks surrounding the well. Hedges heard the bucket at the end of the rope splash into water as he dived from the saddle, sliding the Spencer from the boot.

'Could've killed you iffen I was of a mind,' the woman went on in the same tone. 'I'll kill any man as tries anythin'.'

Hedges was crouched on the far side of the well from the house. He peered under his horse's belly into a glassless window. But it was too murky inside the house for him to see anything. He glanced at the group of mounted men. Every one was holding a levelled rifle or handgun.

'Sounds like an old biddy, sir!' Forrest called.

'Old of limb but keen of eye, you trespassing varmints!' the woman snapped in reply.

Hedges waved a hand, palm down, towards the men. 'Place looked deserted, ma'am,' he shouted.

'Things ain't always what they look. Get back on your horse and ride out of here. Battle's over and we want some peace.'

Seward ignored Hedges' signal to hold still. He hooked up a leg, intent upon sliding from the saddle and making a run for the side of the house. A second shot blasted out of the house – from the window on the other side of the door.

'Friggin' hell!' the baby-faced youngster yelled, and re-sat his saddle as the bullet cracked past his head.

'Do like my grandma told you!' This from another

woman, who was much younger and sounded a great deal more afraid.

Hedges scowled at Seward, then looked back at the house. 'Who won the battle?'

'Don't know and don't care. Me and Betsy ain't in the war.'

'Is this Federal or Confederate territory?' Hedges tried again.

'Don't know or care. Just happy neither the Yankees nor the Rebs tried to stop me and Betsy comin' back here last night. Be happier still iffen you bunch move on out.'

Hedges knew he had to take a risk and that all he had going for him was the fact that neither woman had shot to kill. He had to put the men's lives on the line too, but Forrest – if none of the others – would recognise that he was taking the larger risk. And the Sergeant would hold the men in check. So he stood up and moved out of the cover of the well and his horse.

'What the – ' Scott rasped.

'We mean you no harm, ma'am,' Hedges said, and allowed the Spencer to drop to the ground. 'Only need some food, water and rest.' He unbuckled his gunbelt and allowed this to fall atop the rifle. 'Going to come up to the door and knock. You open the door, the others will drop their guns. No objection to you and Betsy keeping yours.'

He started to walk forward, squinting in the first rays of the sun shafting across the burnt out country from the east.

'I can plug you right in the heart, young feller!' the old woman warned.

But she didn't, and then he was at the door and he let out his pent-up breath. There was no stoop. He clenched a fist and thudded his knuckles on the bullet-pitted wood. He sensed the men staring at his back, searching for a signal.

'They drop the guns before I open up!' the old woman said to end the long, tense pause which followed the knock.

'Do it, Forrest,' Hedges said, not turning around.

'I don't like it,' the Sergeant growled.

'What *do* you like?' Hedges answered.

Then he got support from an unlikely quarter.

'I'm with the Captain,' Rhett said suddenly, letting fall his Colt and hooking the Spencer from the boot to drop it to the ground. 'Two women ain't gonna gun down seven unarmed men.'

Forrest spat. 'What we got to lose except our friggin' lives?' he snarled, and tossed away his guns.

'One thing, young feller!' the old woman called as the other men discarded their weapons.

'What's that?' Hedges replied as footfalls creaked floorboard inside.

Then the door swung open and he looked at a frailly-built, sunken-cheeked, hard-eyed woman who was in her seventies at least. But she was far from senile. The Starr rifle she aimed at his heart was rock steady.

'I don't allow no foul language in my house,' she warned.

'They'll act seemly, ma'am,' Hedges promised, reaching out to grasp the barrel of the Starr.

'That's an oath if even I friggin' heard one,' Rhett said with a guffaw.

'What you doin'?' Betsy said as the old woman tried to jerk the rifle away from Hedges.

She was in her late teens and had the basis of prettiness, spoiled by her painful thinness. A shapeless denim dress with many stains atop its original blue colour suggested that her body was as sparse as her face. She thrust a matching Starr rifle at the doorway.

'Just don't like guns aimed at me,' Hedges said evenly as the men moved up behind him.

'I'll kill you!' Betsy menaced, the flush of anger adding colour to her hollow cheeks.

'Aw, he knows,' the old lady moaned, and surrendered the gun.

Hedges showed his cold grin. 'Got a gun just like these two back home in Iowa. Single shot. Know how long it takes to reload and the kind of noise you make doing it.'

'Well, how about that?' Seward rasped.

'All yours if you want it, Billy,' Forrest allowed. 'One's too skinny and the other's too old.'

'I didn't – ' Seward started.

The young girl delved a hand into a pocket of her shapeless dress and snatched out a shell. Hedges reached her before she had even got the breech open. She screamed as he jerked the rifle away from her.

'Don't you – ' This time it was the old lady who started a sentence that was stillborn. But it was the Captain's words, rather than his actions, which curtailed the protest.

'No cussin' or anything else in this house – except what I tell you to do!' he snarled. His narrowed blue eyes raked the grizzled faces of the men. Then he moderated his tone, but the quiet words had more menace than if he had bellowed them. 'Unless the Rebs have got Washington, we're a spit from home and dry.'

'I just meant how about these dames gettin' us to toss away our guns with empty rifles, for Chris . . . for goodness sake,' Seward complained, cutting in on the Captain.

'Could've been worse, Billy,' Forrest muttered with a grin. 'Could've used their feminine charm.'

Although his mouth showed humour, his eyes swung between the women with a glint of contempt for them. Patiently, Hedges controlled his ice-cold anger.

'Home and dry,' he continued, 'I'll court-martial any man who disobeys an order from here on in.'

He treated each man to another glinting stare, and drew impassiveness for a response. Then Rhett broke the uneasy silence.

'You won't get no trouble from me, sir,' he said.

'So long as the Captain keeps his back to the wall,' Bell taunted.

The humour was weak, but the men used it as an excuse to shatter the tension with hollow laughter.

'I'm obliged to you, mister,' the old lady said, almost gently, after Hedges had ordered the men to retrieve their weapons and attend to their horses. 'I figured me and Betsy were in for a bad time, for sure.'

Hedges eyed both women blankly and he resisted the temptation to match the older one's tone. For he didn't want to give them hope. 'Don't count on them staying the way they are, lady,' he warned coldly. 'Right now, fix some breakfast. A lot of it, and good.'

She ignored the tone and smiled. She had no teeth. 'Sure thing, mister. Come on Betsy. Like I always told your mother and you, the way to a man's heart is through his stomach.'

'Only works if a man's got a heart,' Hedges muttered as the women retreated into the kitchen and he went outside to experience the warm sunlight of the new day.

Out there, as he unsaddled and watered his horse, then ground-hobbled the animal on a patch of grass, he sensed the animosity the men directed tacitly towards him. He thought he knew the reason. Basically undisciplined, the men had been little more than a murdering, robbing, raping mob for too long. He had reminded them that they would soon be back in uniform again, exposed to formal military authority. For months they had wanted nothing better than to get out of Rebel-held territory – and Forrest's uncertainty about whether he himself could lead them to safety was the chief reason he had given his reluctant backing to Hedges. But, now that they were within sight of their goal, they could visualise more clearly what awaited them there. And Hedges' threat of a court-martial had brought the future into even sharper focus. So, what might have been gratitude and admiration for him – albeit grudging from such men as these – was actually sourness.

But, under the influence of the simple, large and well-cooked meal which Betsy and her grandmother served, the mood of the men underwent another change. As they ate they became mellower and then the luxury of good food in combination with the utter peace of the surroundings heightened their weariness and each man chose his spot and bedded down.

As the sound of stentorian snoring disturbed the peace of the house, Hedges moved a chair to a north-facing window and slumped into it. He was still concerned about the subject of the men's muttering together as they tended to their horses. But all he could do was stay alert for any move they intended to make, and the sounds of their deep sleeping indicated that would be several hours in coming. So he just gazed fixedly into the north across the scarred battleground of The Wilderness and allowed himself the hope that future battles would be few. For he could see the old woman working in the overgrown turnip field and he visualised Jamie tending to the chores on their farmstead in the heart of Iowa.

He realised he had never been so sick of the war: so sick, he was loathed to admit, that he was even prepared to accept a Confederate victory if it meant he could return quickly to his brother and the farmstead. For, like the men, he no longer had any clear conviction about the cause in whose name he was fighting. And, ignoring this, he had witnessed, experienced – suffered from and taken part in – brutal acts on both the Confederate and the Federal side. So, in such a war, God could be an ally of neither side. Not that he believed in a God anymore: and in a Civil War patriotism played no part. So there was nothing worth fighting for.

His view across the ravaged country grew as fuzzed as his thinking and he became another willing victim of sleep.

Betsy screamed. Hedges was jerked into awareness and, with the lessons of war well learned, he had total recall. He heard only the final remnant of the scream, but he recognised that it was vented by a woman. And through the glassless window he saw the old one hurl away her hoe and pick up her skirts to run towards the house. He saw the desperate anxiety in her ancient face but knew it was not she who had screamed. He also knew, from the position of the fierce summer sun, that he had slept into the mid-afternoon.

This complete orientation to his surroundings and their condition took only part of a second. Then he was on his feet, Spencer snatched from where it leaned against the wall. He pumped a shell into the breech as he raced across the tiny room and jerked open the door. Men were coming out of other doorways, rubbing sleep from their eyes, yelling questions and fumbling with clothing and guns.

One raking glance with his slitted eyes told Hedges who was missing. He saw Forrest and Seward coming fast out of one bedroom, Bell emerging from another, Scott rising from the hallway floor and Rhett stumbling in through the back door of the house.

'Captain, riders comin'!' Rhett yelled in high excitement. 'They look like – '

Scott reached the door of the kitchen a moment before Hedges and flung it wide. The two leaders were bundled through by the pressure of the other men at the back. They all skidded to a halt, the men at the rear jostling to see past those at the front.

'They look like Union,' Rhett completed, his voice cracking.

Nobody was listening to him.

Douglas, dressed only in pants and undervest, had Betsy arched backwards across a scrubbed pine table. She was partially nude to the waist, where her attacker had ripped away the dress at one side. The nails of his clawed fingers had gouged three bloody ruts in her bare flesh, from the shoulder to the nipple of the just discernible swell of her exposed, developing breast. Terror screamed tacitly from her bulging eyes, but one of Douglas' hands was clamped over her mouth to hold back further screams. His other hand was struggling to completely uncover her upper body. She had ceased to offer physical resistence and was clutching at a cheap metal crucifix hung around her neck on a cord. She held it high, on a level with the man's lust-gleaming eyes.

'Corporal!' Hedges roared, and sent a rifle shot crashing towards the kitchen ceiling.

But there were cooking pots hanging from an overhead beam. The bullet clanged against the bottom of one and ricochetted. It angled downward and burst into the slack skin of the old woman's throat as she showed her horrified face at the kitchen window. She died instantly and was thrown backwards by the impact. Now horror was etched into the hawkish features of Hedges as he stared at the bright splash of blood on the ledge of the glassless window. He was blind to all else as remorse for the fatal accident froze him into a harrowing state of suspended animation.

Douglas leapt away from the young girl, who went down into a squat on the floor and began to vent body-shaking sobs as she kissed the crucifix. The corporal's action brought him between Hedges and the blood-stained window ledge and he had no reason to believe that the ice-cold look in the eyes of the grief-stricken man was not directed at him.

'Tell him, Frank!' Douglas pleaded as hoofbeats trembled the hot afternoon air. 'Back me, you guys. Tell him we agreed. Tell him we don't give a shit for his orders. Any of us. Tell him you all said it was all right for me to have her.'

'Company comin', Frank,' Billy Seward said urgently, pumping the action of his Spencer.

Rhett raced back to the kitchen after making a hurried check on the approaching riders. 'It's like I said!' he shrieked in delight. 'Union! A whole friggin' cavalry troop! We're saved!'

'Frank!' Douglas yelled.

Betsy sobbed, dropping forward out of her squat to adopt a kneeling position. The crucifix was held between her praying hands.

'We didn't agree nothin',' Forrest snarled, and drew his Colt as the sound of the approaching cavalry troop swelled. 'Right, you guys?'

'Not me,' Scott said.

'Nor me.' From Bell.

'You're crazy, Hal,' Seward accused.

Rhett shrugged. 'Guess not, Sergeant.'

'What they call unanimous,' Forrest proclaimed with a curt nod. Then he aimed the Colt and squeezed the trigger.

The second shot jerked Hedges out of the trance-like condition into which the result of the first one had plunged him. He saw the terrified Douglas, then glanced to the side in time to see Betsy die. Her frail, semi-nude body was sent crashing to the floor. Her pasty face was curtained by a welter of blood streaming from the entry and exit holes of the bullet at each temple. Then he swung to the side still further: and watched Forrest toss the smoking Colt at the body, snatch Seward's Spencer from him and hurl this over to the floor under the window with the blood-splashed ledge.

The Sergeant trapped the Captain's eyes in a level stare that was at once quizzical and challenging.

'Federal cavalry troop outside, sir,' Forrest reported tersely. 'Looks like we're home and dry. Been a damn shame these two Reb dames had blasted us right at the last.'

'Frank?' Douglas yelled.

'Shuddup, Corporal!' Forrest snarled.

Hedges, all his senses functioning once more, looked quickly at each man in turn. Only Rhett expressed his joy at the arrival of the uniformed troopers. Forrest's eyes continued to taunt. Seward, Bell and Scott were merely expectant. Douglas was still afraid.

'They said they'd back me, sir,' he croaked.

The Captain recalled the mutterings of the early morning and then, fleetingly, remembered older events: isolated incidents which had shown the men's resentment towards Douglas because he was unfitted to wear his chevrons.

'Toss up which one of us they hate the most, Corporal,' he replied sourly.

'So what you figure to do about it, Captain?' Forrest asked as the horsemen broke from an orderly column to surround the house.

'Whoever's in there, come on out with your hands high!'

The commanding voice sounded from the front of the house. Troopers, recently shaved, and garbed in newly-pressed uniforms with shining buttons, appeared beyond the kitchen window.

'Well, Captain?' Forrest urged.

'What the man says – for now,' Hedges replied, pushing his Spencer on to the pine table and starting to unbuckle his gunbelt.

'Never thought I'd be happy to get captured, for Christsake!' Rhett muttered as he and the other's disarmed themselves.

'Captain ordered no cussin', Bob,' Seward reminded.

Forrest glanced at Hedges and saw he was looking at the slumped body of the young girl. One of her arms was outstretched, the hand opened to show the metal cross lying in the palm.

'Reckon he's thinkin' some real mean things himself right now,' the Sergeant growled.

Hedges showed the non-com a cold grin that parted his thin lips without reaching his narrowed eyes. 'No, Forrest,' he rasped. 'Just something a little different from what my Ma used to say a lot. Just Betsy's to heaven.'

Edge was no longer the sheriff of Monksville, but he remained in the law office as the cold night slid through into the colder early hours of a new day. From the point of view of the citizens, perhaps it was because they were all – from the mayor down – afraid to try and evict him. Or perhaps it was because they just didn't care. The only other survivor of those who had caused trouble to explode in the law-abiding community was Melody Devine. And she was still unconscious from the bullet wound, held in bed and under guard at Doc Hartmann's house.

The half-breed stayed in the warm office because he had committed himself to awaiting the arrival of the Kansas lawman and it was a comfortable place to kill the time. Since no move was made to get him out, he didn't consider what counter-action he might take. He just sat, with the stove glowing and the lamp turned down, alternately reading the telegraph and staring morosely into space. He smoked a lot of cigarettes – and was midway through another when he heard the clop of hooves coming down the trail from the north. The approaching rider held his horse to a weary walk and Edge had time to smoke the cigarette at a measured pace before the newcomer moved into the square.

The horse was reined to a halt and the half-breed eased out of his chair, canted the Winchester across his shoulder and ambled to the door. He pulled it open and felt again the bite of the night air on his stubbled face. The brightness of the moonlight seemed to intensify the cold.

'So the telegraph brought you running, Edge?' the horseman said flatly. 'Remember me?'

He was no more than five feet six inches tall and sparsely

built. His face had regular features that merged into a kind of nondescript handsomeness. At first impression a forgettable man, garbed in a well-fitting, high-priced eastern suit topped by a low-crowned hat. But the half-breed knew the way in which the man could get a certain look into his coal-black eyes and put a slight twist on his mouth to leave a lasting impression on all who saw him in such circumstances. The expression was a kind of quarter smile, with menace monopolising the other seventy-five per cent of the look. Men were either warned off by the look, or ignored it at risk of being blasted into eternity by the gunfighter's Remington revolver or Martini-Henry rifle.

That was in the old days. There had been at least one change since then. The tin star on his jacket lapel displayed the fact that he was no longer a gunfighter.

'Who could forget Summer, Pike,' Edge replied evenly.

He wasn't talking about the season. Instead, a town in the Dakota Bad Lands where the two men had met and then parted. A town where they had shared a bounty but where Edge had beaten Pike for the love of Elizabeth Day.

Perhaps later, the half-breed thought, he might wonder why he had not realised Pike was behind the telegraph. Because re-awakened memories of Beth excluded all else but the woman herself? He set aside the question for later consideration. Faced by a man like Pike, he needed to stay totally alert to the present.

'It was just luck I found that old wanted poster on you when I got the sheriff's job,' Pike said. 'Just a couple of days after I heard about the way you let Elizabeth die. It didn't take luck to find you.'

'You must have wanted to real bad.'

'You can guess why?'

Edge nodded. 'I reckon. Personal reasons.'

Now Pike nodded. 'Real personal. It's why I needed to pin you down someplace outside my jurisdiction.'

'I figured.'

'Nancy didn't tell you?'

Pike was sitting easily on his weary horse, hands still holding the reins, far from the holstered Remington and booted

Martini-Henry. Edge, aware of the man's speed, poised himself to get rid of the uncocked Winchester and go for his Colt.

'She didn't say much at all. But what she did say got her in trouble. The worst kind.'

He saw the slightly-built lawman become suddenly tense, but read the switch accurately. Pike was preparing to make his move. He wasn't making it yet.

'What's that mean, Edge?' he rasped.

The courthouse clock struck a solemn note to mark the hour of one.

'Along with a few others, tomorrow she'll be buried.'

The shock slowed Pike fractionally. He released the reins as fast as Edge dropped the rifle. But the Colt was coming out of the holster ahead of the Remington.

Neither handgun exploded. Instead, there was a deafening barrage of larger calibre bullets belching from the muzzles of rifles. Divots of dirt and puffs of dust rose from around the hooves of the horse. While splinters of wood flew out of the doorframe and up from the sidewalk where Edge stood. The half-breed and the lawman clashed eyes and reached an instantaneous tacit agreement. Their hands left their guns and they raked the square with hard, unafraid stares. The residue of sound from the single fusillade rolled away into the vast emptiness of Death Valley.

'We've had enough!' Scott Gerstenberg bellowed from cover. 'Monksville don't want any more killin'. You guys got somethin' to settle, go someplace else.'

The shots had come from all around the square, high up and low down. The riflemen had had a long, cold wait in secure cover. And they didn't show themselves now. All the two men in the open could be sure of was that the angry mayor was in the church.

'Or you'll kill us?' Pike called.

'Ain't how we want to end it, but we're ready, if that's what you want.' There was the unmistakable sound of a shell being pumped into the breach of a lever action rifle. Then a whole chorus of similar sounds from all around the square.

'I'm easy,' Pike said softly.

Edge grinned coldly. 'You're too modest, feller.'

Pike wiped the back of a hand across his mouth. 'You're easier. Call it.'

'Ain't what we want to do, friend, but somehow it's got to end!' Gerstenberg called.

'Poetic, ain't he?' Edge posed.

'Come on, Edge, he sounds like he knows what he's talking about,' Pike urged.

The half-breed nodded. 'Sure knows the verse. We'll move out. Got to give him and everybody else another chapter.'

CHAPTER SEVEN

THE blood-run face of the old woman haunted Hedges throughout the remainder of the war. The image of her dying was strong in his mind as he and his men were escorted, under open arrest, to Federal Army headquarters in Washington. It was even stronger during the month-long period into mid-August when, after their identities were established, the men were given a furlough. While Forrest and the others spent the time drinking and whoring around the city's low spots, frittering away their accumulated back pay, Hedges checked into a Pennsylvania Avenue Hotel that was neither the best nor the worst Washington had to offer.

He did only one constructive thing – mailed home to Jamie the bulk of his pay. The balance paid the rent for his room and a constant supply of rye whiskey. While the battles of Peachtree Creek and Crater were fought far to the south, and Admiral Farragut won the Battle of Mobile Bay for the Union, Captain Josiah C. Hedges drank and slept. And he had hallucinations and nightmares about the face at the window of the tiny farmhouse in the ravaged wilderness.

It took three staff officers an entire day to sober him up to a point where he could understand that he had received a commendation from General Ulysses S. Grant. This was in recognition of the attempt to assassinate the Confederate President and for successfully leading his unit of troopers back to safety. There was then a week for Hedges to regain complete equilibrium and for the men to be rounded-up before the parade at which Grant personally presented the honour.

Then the big push to Atlanta got underway. Hedges was given command of a full cavalry troop, all of the men as experienced and hard-bitten as the six who had fought under him for so long. The troop was assigned to the army of General William T. Sherman and were with him when he smashed his way into Atlanta. They took part in the ruthless evacuation of civilians from the city and then did more than their share of the fire-raising that left Atlanta little more than a burned-out shell.

The memory of the old woman faded in Hedges' mind as he watched his own troopers and the men commanded by other officers re-affirm their places in hell. In full-scale battles and unimportant skirmishes, and during the long, brutal march to the sea at Savannah he witnessed slaughter so harrowing that the death of one old woman became insignificant. But then came a two-month period of relative calm, from Christmas 1864 until the mid-February of the New Year when Sherman's army moved out towards a victory at Columbia. And, in that interlude, the accidental killing in The Wilderness weighed heavily on Hedges again. But, at least, the image of the ancient face at the window was growing blurred.

With Georgia and the Carolinas almost secured for the Union, Hedges' troop was among those transferred to the command of General Philip H. Sheridan who was destined to lead his army into the final major campaign of the War Between The States.

March ran its course and April opened. Sheridan's cavalry came down from the Shenandoah Valley and the transferees from Sherman's army joined the near twelve thousand mounted men at Dinwiddie Court House. And, on April Fool's Day, the massive well armed and well-provisioned column moved out to take the important road junction and railroad link known as Five Forks.

Hedges' troop formed a part of the left flank attack and the men were in high spirits as they cantered their horses across the soft-textured Virginia countryside under a warm spring sun.

'Hear tell this war's gonna be over and done before the end of the month,' a tall, thin corporal said to his neighbour.

'Make's a friggin' change from Christmas,' a sergeant at his side answered, but without sourness.

Rhett, riding ahead of the two men, grinned at Bell beside

him. 'You reckon that's right, Rog?' he asked. 'I been hearin' a lot of that talk.'

'Could be,' Bell replied.

'Yeah,' Seward called over his shoulder. 'Could be the last chance you'll get to blast guys in the back and not hang for it, Bob.'

But nothing could deflate the New Englander's optimistic mood concerning the strong rumours that the war was drawing to an end. 'Only way you can blast the Johnnie Rebs, Billy,' he shouted. 'On account of they're always runnin' away when we show up.'

Riding out at the head of the column, just in front of Forrest and Douglas, Hedges did not order the men into silence. As a mere Captain, with a field rather than a staff command, he had received no official briefing on the state of the war. But he had heard the same rumours as the non-coms and enlisted men: rumours that were so strong they had to be true. However, he knew that a soldier had as much chance of dying in the final battle of a war as in the opening one. And, if a man was destined to be killed, it was good he should be in high-spirits before it happened. So he allowed the bantering to continue, aware that the men's good mood would not detract from their determination to give of their best in the coming fight. Rather, their belief that this could be the final opportunity to slaughter with impunity would act as a spur to such men as these.

The major commanding the left flank of the attacking forces ordered a halt, but there was no dismount. The men sat in their saddles and looked with excited expectation towards the cluster of buildings that squatted around a crossroads to the north. Beyond Five Forks they could just make out the tracks of the Southside Railroad which was the Rebel supply route they were required to cut. In front of the tiny community of such strategic importance, the Confederate army under General Pickett was dug in.

The opposing armies faced each other, out of firing range, and waited. Noon came and the Union men grew disgruntled with the inactivity. Hedges cursed as much as anybody, aware that with each passing minute, the men's fighting edge was being blunted. Then word came to dismount and eat. The messengers who delivered this order also carried, unofficially, the news that Phil Sheridan was awaiting reinforcements in the shape of a corps under the command of Brigadier General G. K. Warren, who had been ordered to Five Forks by Grant.

'What you think, Captain?' Forrest asked with a half-grin as the two men finished eating and smoked cigarettes, both peering out towards the objective.

Hedges spat. 'That Sheridan ain't as hot as he's cracked up to be, sergeant.'

Forrest's grin expanded into a harsh laugh. 'Reckon we got the makin's of a paint-Phil-yellow-club here, sir. We could send them Rebs on the run with half the men we already got.'

'But that ain't our decision, is it?' Hedges grunted, and fixed the Sergeant with a warning stare.

Now Forrest spat, and added a shrug. 'More's the friggin' pity. This war could've been over years ago if they'd picked the right guys for the generals.'

Hedges showed a frosty grin. 'That sounds almost like a compliment, Sergeant,' he growled.

Forrest looked away, out of the trees in which they were waiting and towards the strongly defended community. 'I've had respect for a lot of guys I've killed,' he said evenly. 'You've done good in this war. We both know that, 'cause we're both still alive.'

'You'll have me weeping on your shoulder in a minute, Forrest,' Hedges told him. 'I get your point, and thanks. Now get back to where you belong before they start talking about us.'

The Sergeant stood up with a nod. Then he grinned again. 'Got no worries there, sir. Every man in the troop knows Rhett's the only guy they got to take rearguard action against.'

'Whereas we see every side of a man except one, uh?'

Forrest looked perplexed, then laughed. 'Right, Captain,' he agreed. 'You got a lot of sides that interest me. But not the back.'

'Get there,' Hedges ordered, and jerked his thumb towards where the troopers were finishing their meal deeper in the timber.

Forrest rejoined the men and Hedges continued his survey of the Confederate defences of Five Forks. But his thoughts were not concerned with planning a strategy to beat the Rebels, for such scheming was not up to him. Instead, he stared at the arena of the battle to come and wondered if the events to take place there would once and for all wipe out the dimming memory of the old woman he had killed. Or whether, if he survived the battle and it proved in fact to be the final fighting in the war, he would carry to his death the haunting image of her dying face. As a punishment, perhaps, for the brutality and atrocities he had committed or condoned in the name of a long-forgotten cause.

Then, at mid-afternoon, as the messengers sprinted away from Sheridan's command post, the Federal artillery barrage opened up: and there was no time for remembering the past or contemplating the future. The orders were delivered to the subordinate commanders and the battle was on. Warren's corps had failed to arrive and Sheridan had sensed the demoralising effect the waiting was having on his men.

'Mount 'em up, Captain?' Forrest yelled above the deafening roar of the big guns screaming cannon-shot, shells and mortar bombs into the Rebel positions.

He had seen Hedges listening to the breathless words of a runner and waited until the corporal had sprinted off before anticipating the order. For a few moments, Hedges said nothing. He simply went to where his horse was tethered and slid his newly-issued Henry rifle from the saddle-boot. Then he unbuttoned his holster flap and drew his sabre before facing the expectant faces of his men.

'Seems Sheridan's sick of the saddle!' he yelled. 'We're back acting like infantry again. Let's move!'

He whirled and broke into a fast run out of the trees, sabre extended in front of him. All along the front, other junior officers were setting the same example to their men:

racing out of solid cover towards the insubstantial screening of smoke and spraying dirt exploded by the heavy artillery barrage. And, behind each leading man, the toopers turned foot-soldiers burst into sight, venting full-throated battle-cries to add to the din of the big guns. Within moments, the crack of small arms fire augmented the tumult of war. The Rebel picket lines fired first, the men panicked by the weight of the advancing army.

Blue-uniformed figures pitched to the broken terrain in welters of blood, and the tone of their comrades' yells altered from excitation to anger. Without waiting for the order, Union troops sent rifle and revolver fire towards the Rebels' advance positions. Hedges was among them. He saw a young lieutenant, twenty yards on his left, take a bullet in the leg and begin to tumble. Before the officer hit the ground, two more bullets had ripped into him. Blood sprayed from his right ear and throat as his scream of agony ended. Hedges felt nothing personally for the lieutenant. The death of the man merely acted to trigger the familiar exhilaration of battle. All else before this had been too remote. But now death had struck close at hand and released adrenalin to power through Hedges' body.

Without breaking from the run, he thrust the sabre into its scabbard and started to rake the Henry back and forth, pumping the action and squeezing the trigger. Other men joined in the wild firing and made it effective. Rebel pickets, safe from the artillery barrage which arced over their heads, leapt from their dug-outs and turned tail from the hail of lead exploding out of the seemingly solid wall of blue-uniformed figures racing towards them.

Hedges saw a dozen Rebels pitch to the ground with ghastly red patches blossoming on their backs. He didn't know whether any of his own bullets had found a human target. His first chance of a certain kill came as he dived into a dug-out in which four Rebel pickets had been positioned. Only one was there now: a boy no older than seventeen who was crouched in a corner, crying with terror and stinking from when he had fouled himself as the attack was launched.

'Please don't kill me, sir?' he begged, pressing himself close against the moist earth. He threw his rifle at Hedges' feet.

Two other blue-uniformed figures lunged into the dug-out as more big guns exploded their full-throated roars across the battlefield. Great clods of earth exploded from the surrounding ground to show that the new barrage came from the Confederate artillery.

'I've been a prisoner, kid,' Hedges grunted as he ducked under the spraying dirt. 'You wouldn't like it.'

But it was Forrest's Colt that exploded before Hedges could bring the Henry to bear. The centre of the kid's forehead exploded blood and shattered bone and he became an inert pile in the corner of the dug-out.

'You said he wouldn't like being no prisoner, Captain!' Seward yelled in defence of Forrest as all three squatted to reload.

'The Sergeant's real helpful,' Hedges muttered.

'Just wouldn't like for you to have no more innocent victims on your conscience, sir,' Forrest said with an evil grin.

Hedges shot a narrow-eyed glance at him and the Sergeant shrugged. Then all three threw themselves full length on the bottom of the dug-out as two exploding shells hurled dirt and twisted metal at them.

'Brought a dame up to your hotel room back in Washington, Captain,' Forrest said in a low voice as they rose, brushing dirt from their heads. 'But you were smashed out of your mind and rantin' about another dame. Killin' that kid wouldn't have helped none.'

Then he was up and out of the dug-out, zig-zagging fast through the drifting smoke and the whining bullets. Seward was hard on his heels and Hedges saw other men going full-tilt into the advance. He recognised many from his own troop – Rhett, Scott and Douglas among others.

'You bastard!' he rasped, directing his hatred at Forrest as he clawed up out of the trench and joined the charge again.

It was obvious the Sergeant thought he was cracking

up and he resented this. Resented it primarily because he had his own doubts about his state of mind but thought he had been able to hide this from the men. But Forrest knew, and maybe he had put out the word to the others. Or perhaps they had even reached the conclusion on their own. Since that month-long drunk in Washington, Hedges had fought in much the same manner as when he was a raw lieutenant at the start of the war: killing as a last resort and only when it was absolutely necessary. All the men in his troop could well have noticed this. And, if they had, it would not be long before Forrest would claim a victory over him. It was even conceivable that Forrest had issued a veiled warning of this back in the trees when he said: *You've done good in this war.* Past tense. Not: *You're doing good.* A warning that the battle of Five Forks was a last chance for Hedges to prove himself the better man.

He lengthened his stride and ran in a straight line to overhaul the men who dodged from left to right to make themselves harder targets. He saw Douglas for the first time since the charge began and thus knew that all six of his war-long comrades were still alive. On seeing the Corporal, he decided to strip the man of his chevrons for allowing himself to be talked into disobeying orders back at the farmstead in The Wildnerness.

But first there was something vastly more important to take care of. Above all else, he had to prove himself – to himself and to the men. He had to prove that the blood-pounding exhilaration was not self-deception. Prove that, had Forrest not taken the life of the terrified, unarmed kid in the dug-out, he would have squeezed the trigger of the Henry. For, as he lunged out ahead of every other Union soldier on the battlefield, he did not know if he would have – could have – killed the boy.

Bullets cracked around him and some even snagged at his uniform. But a volatile mixture of anger, hatred, resentment and self-doubt clouded his sound judgement as effectively as swirling gunsmoke blanketed the battlefield. He ran through the hail of flying lead with utter recklessness, the skin on his lean features stretched taut, his teeth bared and his slitted eyes glinting like strips of bright blue precious gems.

Six Rebel riflemen crouched in a trench saw him lunge out of a pall of black smoke and stared at him as though they thought he was the angel of death. But he was merely the instrument.

He saw the six pale faces from a distance of four feet, and the Henry exploded twice before he leapt over the mound of earth and into the trench. One Rebel took a bullet in his gaping mouth and fragments of his teeth were washed out with a gush of blood. A second was flung back against the rear of the trench, fountaining a crimson cascade from where his right eye had been. Three bullets were crashed towards Hedges, but he was already going down hard into the trench and the shells whined over his head.

The muzzle of the uncocked Henry jabbed forcefully into the throat of the soldier immediately in front of him and the man crumpled, screaming his agony to a high pitch.

Hedges released the rifle and snatched out the Remington revolver with his right hand and the sabre with his left. He was aware of men emerging from the smoke pall, to look down upon him the mound of earth displaced in the digging of the trench. He caught just a glimpse of them: enough to be sure their uniforms were blue. Then he fired the Remington. The single Rebel in front of him took the bullet in his belly, folded forward and sat down hard, dropping his rifle and adding his screams to those from the man clawing at his throat.

'Captain!' Bell's voice.

'Shaddup!' From Forrest.

Hedges whirled. One Rebel was four feet away, levelling a Spiller and Burr sixgun. The other man was behind this one, trying to get a shot from his Sharps. Hedges lunged forward, into a crouch, swinging the sabre. The Rebel's handgun exploded to belch smoke, flash and lead. The bullet struck the chambers of Hedges' Remington and sent the gun spinning out of his numbed hand. Then the sabre's edge slashed across the front of the man's thighs. The man staggered backwards, dropping his gun and crashing into the man behind him. The Sharps exploded to bury a bullet uselessly into the side of the trench. The injured man sank to the ground, losing a massive amount of blood from the gaping wounds in his thighs. Now he began to scream and the venting of agony from the trench covered every other sound of the battle.

The Rebel with the Sharps struggled to wrench the rifle from beneath the weight of the man who had spoiled his aim. But, as he straightened, he died. Hedges had flicked over his wrist and started the sabre on another swing. The blade bit into the side of the man's neck, angling downwards. The blow had enough power to drive the honed edge clean through the flesh and muscle to the top of the spine. Thus, as the dead man fell, his head flopped forward to display a ghastly, blood-frothing wound that drew a cheer from the watchers on the earth pile above.

'Leave 'em!' Hedges heard Forrest snarl as he whirled around to survey the wounded, who continued to scream and groan their agonies.

He saw the men above more clearly now, as his anger turned from hot to cold. And he recognised them as the six men to whom he most desperately wanted to prove himself. He saw Rhett and Seward lower their rifles in response to Forrest's order. Then he devoted his attention to the three surviving Rebels, as the audience sank into comfortable squats.

The man with the slashed thighs was sitting upright, hands clawed over his gaping wounds as if trying to hold the flaps of flesh together. He had his eyes tight closed and so didn't see the sabre driving towards him. The blade went between his arms and sank deep into his stomach. The feel of the metal tearing into his entrails shocked his heart into stopping and his screams ended. Hedges left the sabre buried into the dead flesh and lunged towards his next victim, hand streaking to the back of his neck to draw the razor. This was the Rebel who had felt the Henry muzzle crashing into his throat. He saw the Union Captain coming for him and terror galvanised him into action. He turned and tried to clamber out of the trench. Hedges kept his hand low, then swung it up. The razor flashed between the pumping legs of the would-be escaper. His screams rose an octave as he fell back into the trench. Hedges jerked his hand away and it was slick with bright crimson. The Rebel's hands reached for the source of his greater agony as he fell full-length into the bottom of the trench. This left his bruised throat exposed for Hedges to slash the bloodstained razor across it.

Just the man with a bullet in his belly screamed now. His mouth worked but no words were uttered to punctuate the high-pitched wails. His eyes pleaded for mercy and, for an instant, Hedges almost weakened to extend it to the Rebel. But he sensed the six pairs of excited eyes boring into the back of his neck and this drove him on to finish the job. He brandished the razor to distract the man's attention. Then he launched a powerful kick towards the jaw of the sitting man. The toe of his boot connected with the point of the chin and the head was snapped back with tremendous force. The neck broke with a sharp crack, and it was over.

'Welcome back to the man we know and love,' Forrest rasped.

The words opened up Hedges' ears to the sounds of the battle, which had now moved north towards Five Forks, leaving him and his men behind in a smoke-draped capsule of relative tranquillity – if there could be tranquillity amid so many blood-spilling corpses. He looked up and raked his hooded eyes over the faces of the squatting men. They all wore grins, with subtle admiration visible behind the wryness.

'Captain sure gave that guy somethin' to chew on,' Seward said, nodding to the man who had been shot in the mouth.

'And I reckon that one didn't see things the Captain's way,' Scott said, jabbing his rifle towards the Rebel blasted in the eye.

'Drove that one half out of his head,' Bell added, indicating the man who had been almost decapitated.

Douglas spat at the dead man with the sabre protruding

from his belly. 'Don't think he appreciated the point you made, sir.'

'And he had more than a close shave,' Rhett guffawed, raising a trembling finger towards the Rebel with the cut throat.

Forrest turned his grinning face towards the crumpled body of the soldier with the broken neck. 'Least he got a kick out of it,' he growled.

Hedges drew the sabre from its fleshy resting place and wiped it and the blade of the razor on a uniform of a dead man before sliding the weapons into their accustomed places. Then he retrieved the Henry and the Remington, and checked that the handgun's action still worked despite the dent from the bullet.

'Had your fun?' he asked evenly when all this was done.

'Sure Captain,' Forrest said, extending a hand down into the body-littered trench and hauling Hedges aloft. 'Nothin' me and the boys like better than watchin' an expert at work.' He licked his lips. 'We're glad you still got what it takes.'

Hedges nodded curtly. 'Glad I had an attentive audience.'

'As Shakespeare said, sir, all the world's a stage,' Rhett offered brightly.

'Sure,' Hedges rasped, looking towards Five Forks, where the Union advance was sweeping the Rebels into a disorderly rout. The intervening ground, spread with acrid-smelling, drifting gunsmoke, was humped with the unmoving dead and screaming wounded of both armies. 'Lousy play, ain't it?'

'I reckon it's slayin' 'em,' Seward countered with a giggle.

'We gonna get back into the act, Captain?' Forrest asked.

'Guess so,' Hedges replied, moving off around the trench. 'I take the lead?'

'Who else, sir? You're the one they were all screamin' for.'

EDGE used fifty dollars of his pay as sheriff to buy a horse from the Monksville Livery Stable and then he and Pike were escorted out of town by Gerstenberg and six members of the council. Both men were allowed to keep their weapons because, by tacit agreement, the old-timers forming the escort decided it would be unwise – probably dangerous – to try to disarm them.

It was a slow, cold ride up into the Funeral Mountains and the mayor did not call a halt until the group had put two miles and a high ridge between it and the town. Here, at the centre of a small plateau, he reined his horse and turned in the saddle.

'If this place suits you men, it suits us,' he announced, his breath turning to grey vapour. 'Out of sight of town and none of the folks back there'll hear anythin' that goes on up here.'

Edge glanced around, blowing on his hands. 'Ain't often I get the choice of where to kill a man,' he muttered.

Pike eyed him levelly. 'It'll do,' he said.

Gerstenberg nodded. 'Obliged the way you co-operated with us, young feller,' he said to Pike. Then he glowered at the half-breed. 'Can't bring myself to thank a man like you.'

'You paid what you owed me,' Edge told him flatly.

'Let's get outta here, Scott,' the town treasurer urged, wheeling his horse.

Gerstenberg broke his eyes away from the trap of Edge's impassive stare and thudded in his heels, jerking on the reins. His horse turned to trot back along the tracks left on the ride out and the other members of the council fell in behind him.

Edge and Pike were left, sitting astride their mounts, six feet apart, at the centre of the plateau. The surface for a quarter of a mile in every direction was absolutely flat, dust-layered and completely lacking in any kind of cover. The moon shed a clear, unmoving light on the featureless terrain.

'Tell you something,' Edge said when they had both made another survey of their surroundings.

'What?'

'Sit here for long, we'll both be dead. Frozen clear through.'

Pike had donned buck skin gloves during the ride out. He flexed his fingers in them. 'Without witnesses, you're likely to plug me in the back,' he accused.

Edge flicked a glance towards where the senior citizens of Monksville were disappearing over the rim of the plateau to the west. 'Witnesses wouldn't make any difference,' he answered.

Pike stared hard at him, incredulous at first: then contemptuous. 'I guess it wouldn't.' He spat into the dusty ground between them. 'Okay, we sidle our horses away.'

The half-breed neither voiced nor nodded agreement. And, when Pike began to move his mount to the side, Edge and his newly-purchased horse remained like statues. Anger flared in the lawman's coal-black eyes and Edge concealed his own feelings behind an impassive mask.

'Move, you bastard!' Pike roared.

'Okay,' Edge said.

Pike's hands were still busy with controlling the reins while his legs augmented the instructions to the horse. His mind was boiling with hot anger. Edge, ice-cold and poised, had only to release his reins, draw, cock and fire the Colt. This was the move he made, the combination blurred into a single, fluid action. Pike had to overcome the surprise of the unexpected and alter his physical responses, both with a brain in a turmoil of rage. Even so, he was fast. His Remington was clear of the holster and cocked as Edge's Colt was levelled and fired. The bullet crashed into Pike's wrist and burst clear on the far side after smashing the joint. The Remington dropped to the ground and blood rained down to stain the dust around it.

Pain contorted the lawman's features. The physical kind, from the searing agony in his wrist, and worse – the mental sort from knowing he had failed to do what was so desperately important to him. He groaned and made the effort to die while still trying to complete his mission. He fumbled awkwardly with his left hand in an attempt to slide out the Martini-Henry. Edge allowed him to draw the rifle half out of the boot. Then he squeezed the Colt's trigger a second time. Not at the man. The trigger and part of the guard was blasted away from the rifle. Pike grunted and snatched away his hand. The rifle slid back into the boot.

Rage caught fire inside him again, and burned the misery out of his eyes. 'All right, you wife-murdering half-breed!' he yelled. 'Quit playing games! Put one in me!'

'I didn't kill her,' Edge said flatly.

'You could have saved her!' Pike challenged.

Edge remained icy cold. 'Words won't change how either of us feel, feller. It's over. Ride.'

Pike gulped. 'Ride? Which way? You're letting me go?'

'Maybe. Or maybe I'll shoot you in the back. You're owed a bullet the hard way for using Beth's name for this lousy stunt.'

'I loved – '

'I told you,' Edge cut in, eyes narrowing to glinting slits. 'Words won't change anything.'

Pike became as cold as Edge and the two men sent matching stares at each other. Then the lawman showed his crooked grin. 'Next time, Edge,' he warned, and wheeled his horse. He looked back over his shoulder. 'And there'll be a next time. Because you can't shoot an unarmed man. So you sure as hell can't shoot a man in the back.'

Then he thudded in his heels and his horse lunged into a gallop. He held the reins in his left hand while his right hung low at his side, leaving a trail of blood splashes. Edge watched him, unmoving for a few moments. Then he holstered the Colt and drew the Winchester from the boot. He pumped the action and thudded the stock into his shoulder. With his cheek against the cold wood, he sighted along the barrel, drawing a perfect bead on the back of the retreating Pike.

But it was the same as when he had been facing the slightly-built lawman. It was crazy, but his actions were influenced by the convictions of the other man. He *was* responsible for Beth's death. And, even crazier, if Beth had chosen to marry Pike instead of himself, she would still be alive.

He allowed the Winchester to sag, until it was aimed at the blood-spotted ground. But Pike didn't know this. Nor could the Kansas lawman be certain Edge would not put a bullet in his back. So, when a six foot wide chasm appeared across the path of his galloping horse, he thudded in his heels and tugged at the reins to urge the animal into a leap.

But the gelding was still suffering from the exhaustion of the long ride to Monksville. The headlong gallop had weakened him still more and the jump demanded his final ounce of stamina. His forelegs came up and stretched out, but his hindlegs collapsed with the torment of pulled ligaments as he tried to power forward. With a high-pitched snort of pain, the gelding writhed as he struggled for a footing where there was none. His thrashing forelegs found only thin air and he tipped over the lip of the chasm.

Pike's scream was louder than the animal's cry of terror, as he kicked free of the stirrups. But then he knew there was no way back and he clung to the neck of the tumbling horse – with a faint hope at the back of his fear-frozen mind that the fall would be short and the animal would cushion him.

But the drop was over two hundred feet to the rocky floor of the chasm, and Pike smashed down first, with the crushing weight of the horse on top of him. There was no pain. Just an end to terror as his skull caved in, spewing blood and brain matter across the rocks. Then the pulp of his insides burst from split-open skin. Finally, the gelding was rent asunder by the force of the impact, and the gore of the man and the animal became merged.

The position of the bright moon shed light into the depths of the chasm and Edge was the first to look down upon the heap of crushed flesh and shattered bone spread over the rocks. Scott Gerstenberg, who had waited below the rim of the plateau to witness the outcome of the feud between the two men, reached the lip of the chasm five minutes later. Not trusting himself to ride too close to the drop, he dismounted and walked forward. Then he drew back in horror at the moonlit scene he looked upon.

'What a way to go!' he rasped. 'When I saw you pointing that rifle, I was sure you was gonna finish him with a bullet in the back.'

Edge shrugged and spat into the chasm. Then he wheeled his horse away. 'So did he, I reckon,' he answered evenly. 'But sometimes you can't stop a man jumping to the wrong conclusion.'

EPILOGUE

CAPTAIN Josiah C. Hedges' war ended on April 9, 1865 at Appomattox Court House, Virginia. His final shot in the War Between The States was fired on the morning of the day when Robert E. Lee surrendered the Army of Northern Virginia to Ulysses S. Grant. His bullet brought a Rebel sharpshooter tumbling out of tree. It was the last of many shots he had fired after the Battle of Five Forks. For, as part of Sheridan's victorious army, his troop blazed the trail west along the route of the Southside Railroad – to Burkville, Farmville and then to Appomattox. Resistance was sporadic, but fierce when it occurred.

His final act while a serving officer in the Union army was to strip Hal Douglas of his corporal's chevrons. It was a private ceremony, with just the two principals, Forrest, Seward, Scott, Bell and Rhett present. Private because, as Hedges told the men, they had fought the war on their own for the most part. It was therefore fitting they should end it so.

Then, after he had distributed the discharge papers to the six ninety-day volunteers who had been soldiers for almost four and a half years, he shook hands with each of the men. And, in the genial atmosphere which surrounded all seven as they acknowledged their new-found freedom, old quarrels and animosities seemed forgotten. Even Douglas' resentment at losing his ranking was swamped by his joy at being a civilian again.

Not until the six were mounted and on the point on riding out of camp did Forrest hint that the past might have an effect on the future.

'Maybe we'll be seein' you, Captain,' he said with the familiar evil smile on his mean face. 'Or maybe we won't.'

'Be your choice, Forrest,' Hedges replied.

Then the six raised their hands in farewell, wheeled their

horses and heeled them into a fast gallop. Hedges watched their dust cloud until it faded from sight, then sighed.

'I'll be looking for you,' he muttered. 'But I hope I never see you.'

He was soon to change his mind.

* * *

*JAMIE Hedges counted six riders and there should have been only one. But Joe was surely among them and so he didn't worry for he would willingly shout aloud his happiness to the whole re-united USA if that was the way it had to be. His brother was coming back home after more than five years away at the war and Jamie did not care whether five men or five million were there to witness his jubilation at the event.**

THE END

* This is the opening paragraph of the first book in this series – *Edge: The Loner.*